SHERLOCK HOLMES™ and the July Crisis: A lost novel

By Sir Arthur Conan Doyle
and James Carlopio, BA, MA, PhD

Paperback ISBN 978-1-78092-870-8
ePub ISBN 978-1-78092-871-5
PDF ISBN 978-1-78092-872-2

Published in the UK by MX Publishing
335 Princess Park Manor, Royal Drive,
London, N11 3GX
www.mxpublishing.co.uk
Cover design by www.staunch.com

About the Author

Professor Carlopio is the father of two lovely young ladies, is an itinerant academic, a management consultant and the author of five books on personal growth and development, organisational strategy and change, loves to read and write, and is fortunate enough to live with his amazing partner in a most wonderful country. Visit him at www.jamescarlopio.com

Acknowledgements

Thank you Steve at MX. I appreciate your patience and wisdom. Thank you to Jon Lellenberg, Julie Kelso, and Jeffrey A. Savoye for your help. Thank you to the Poinciana Café in Mullum and the Woodbox Café in West Burleigh as I could never have done this without your wonderful food, tea and surroundings!

My dearest daughters – I love you and wish you, as always … happiness, love and health. The thought of you is never long gone from my mind and heart.

Finally, thank you my dearest Samantha. It is a pleasure, a privilege and an honour to go through life with you.

Contents

Introduction and explanation

What you are about the read is a new Sherlock Holmes story written using the words of Sir Arthur Conan Doyle by me. How is that possible? I will explain: What follows is almost pure Doyle – about 90% pure. Although Doyle was an avid spiritualist, he has not literally come back from the dead ... only figuratively. I have taken words, phrases, sentences, and paragraphs from many of Conan Doyle's 56 short stories and 4 novel-length Sherlock Holmes stories and crafted them into a new story that takes place 100-years-ago in July 1914 just prior to the start of World War I, which is also the 'time' the last of the Holmes stories is set. I have mainly drawn from the *Bruce Partington Plans, The Second Stain*, and *The Naval Treaty*, while borrowing liberally from *A Scandal in Bohemia, His Last Bow, Augustus Milverton* and several others. In order to craft a new story I had to change various characters and events and when this was necessary, I used names and events that are both historically accurate and appropriate given the narrative. The result is a blended kind of historical, editorial fiction. It is at the same time "an adaptation and a creation". If this was a song, it would be a re-mix, rather than a cover-tune.

Some writers, and their characters and stories, are so uniquely entwined with a particular time and/or place, that while others may try to emulate them, the essential character or soul of the original cannot successfully be duplicated or re-created. I think this is the case with Sir Arthur Conan Doyle, Sherlock Holmes and Dr. Watson. While many have tried to re-create the magic, I am always left disappointed. That is what motivated me to create a new story using the words of the master.

While this editorial fiction writing process has, to my knowledge, never before been done with a novel, it is not completely without precedent. I know of two related examples. The first is a play, written and performed first in the late 1800's. William Hooker Gillette, an American actor, playwright and stage-manager, drew material from Doyle's canon, with some dialogue taken from the original stories, and added new material to create his well-loved four-act play. As the plot was largely taken from Conan Doyle, he was credited as a co-author, even though Gillette wrote the play. This is similar to what I have done. According to Starrett's *The private life of Sherlock Holmes,* published in 1933 (p140), "Principally, the play grew out of three celebrated episodes – *A Scandal in Bohemia, The Final Problem,* and *A Study in Scarlet,* in that curiously inverted order – but there are lines and glimpses of certain other tales so skilfully interpolated and so subtly changed as almost to defy the expert. The work is thus at once an adaptation and a creation; and as a whole the credit is largely Gillette's. Certain it is that neither Doyle nor Watson ever saw the manuscript. The play, however, as they have said, delighted them."

The second example is the Cento form of poetry. According to the Academy of American Poet's www.poets.org: "From the Latin word for 'patchwork,' the cento (or collage poem) is a poetic form made up of lines from poems by other poets. Though poets often borrow lines from other writers and mix them in with their own, a true cento is composed entirely of lines from other sources. Early examples can be found in the work of Homer and Virgil." Thus, we may look upon the adaptive creations I have produced, as a weak Cento Novel or as editorial fiction, as I have tried, as my basic "rule" to always use the words of Conan Doyle, or Edgar Allen Poe in the story at the back of this book, wherever possible, and I have credited those great writers with first-authorship as is appropriate. I see what I have done as creative editing, while trying to produce, in the words of Starrett (1933, p 44): "The perfect Holmes adventure, [that] no doubt, would be a shrewd amalgam of the best parts of them all". I am well-aware I have not created the "perfect" Holmes adventure, while I certainly have tried to create a shrewd amalgam of my favourite parts of many of them!

Finally, I must apologize. I apologize first to Sir Arthur Conan Doyle, and his family, and then to you dear reader, for any errors, omissions, inconsistencies, etc. Given the constraints of the task I undertook, I needed to take certain liberties, and to allow myself a good deal of poetic license. For where ever I inevitably do not live up to your expectations, please accept my apologies. When you notice any problems and inconsistencies, will you please excuse me?

If you are a long-time admirer of Conan Doyle and Sherlock Holmes you might like to try and figure out where all the bits and pieces come from. Whether you are a Holmes aficionado or a first-time reader, I hope you enjoy this unique experience.

"But there can be no grave for Sherlock Holmes or Watson...Shall they not always live in Baker Street? … Outside, the hansoms rattle through the rain, and Moriarty plans his latest devilry. Within, the sea-coal flames upon the hearth, and Holmes and Watson take their well-won ease.... So they still live for all that love

3

them well: in a romantic chamber of the heart: in a nostalgic country of the mind: where it is always 1895." [Or, in this case, 1914.]

The Private Life of Sherlock Holmes by Vincent Starrett, 1933 (1993)

Now come with me on a journey of the mind and listen to the voices of old friends fondly remembered …

Prologue

On a visit to Perth, in Western Australia, when I was to meet my new wife's parents for the first time, I made a discovery. My wife's father has led a most unusual life: he left his respectable British home in Rhodesia (Zimbabwe as it is now known) at seventeen, steam-tramped to Europe, made his way through Europe and the Middle-East into Asia, and after many jobs, adventures and mis-adventures, he found himself in Perth. He had recently been back to his family residence, Sandringham House in Norfolk in the UK to visit his brother, and from its basements, as part of his researches with his brother into his family's interesting history, he brought back with him to Australia many documents, books and small items. Knowing I too had an interest in history, and I expect seeking to find some common ground through which we could establish a friendly relationship, he let me have access to these family treasures.

As we companionably sat sorting through the heaps and piles, I happily read documents about their history and when, for example, the family had cared for Elisabeth I during her exile. In the family tree, I found that in later years, some family members were related to Arthur Vicars, Conan Doyle's cousin. In hind-sight, I realise that this must be how I then happened to come upon some yellowed, hand-written papers on which I quickly caught the name 'Sherlock Holmes'. After closer examination, I realised I had found an almost-complete Sherlock Holmes story, written by Sir Arthur Conan Doyle that I have never seen nor even heard of. That document is what you are about to read. It is an unpublished Sherlock Holmes story written by Sir Arthur Conan Doyle that somehow, must have made its way, lost and unregarded, into those family archives.

I am a Sherlock Holmes fan. I first read all the Holmes stories and books when I was in high-school and have re-read, listened and re-listened to them as audio-books many times since. This account of the month proceeding the first World War, and Sherlock Holmes' role in some of the events contributing to it, is as far as I can tell, known to no one and is presented here for the first time in history.

Chapter 1 - Introduction

In recording from time to time some of the curious experiences and interesting recollections which I associate with my long and intimate friendship with Mr. Sherlock Holmes, I have continually been faced by difficulties caused by his own aversion to publicity and in the reluctance which Mr. Holmes has shown to the continued publication of his experiences. So long as he was in actual professional practice the records of his successes were of some practical value to him, but since he has definitely retired from London and betaken himself to study and bee-farming on the Sussex Downs, notoriety has become hateful to him, and he has peremptorily requested that his wishes in this matter should be strictly observed.

To his sombre and cynical spirit all popular applause was always abhorrent, and nothing amused him more at the end of a successful case than to hand over the actual exposure to some orthodox official, and to listen with a mocking smile to the general chorus of misplaced congratulation. It was indeed this attitude upon the part of my friend and certainly not any lack of interesting material which has caused me of late years to lay few of my records before the public.

Mr. Sherlock Holmes was always of opinion that I should eventually publish the singular facts connected with this case, if only to dispel once for all the ugly rumours which some years ago agitated the world and were echoed in London. There were, however, certain obstacles in the way, and the true history of this curious case remained entombed in the tin box which contains so many records of my friend's adventures. It was, then, with considerable surprise that I received a telegram from Homes last Tuesday—he has never been known to write where a telegram would serve—in the following terms:

> Why not tell them of the secret treaty, the French Gold and the Great War - most important case I have mishandled.

I have no idea what sweep of memory had brought the matter fresh to his mind, or what freak had caused him to desire that I should recount it; but I hasten, before another cancelling telegram may arrive, to hunt out the notes which give me the exact details of the case and to lay the narrative before my readers. Now I have at last obtained permission to ventilate the facts which formed the last case handled by Holmes before his retirement from practice. Even now a certain reticence and discretion have to be observed in laying the matter before the public. My participation in some of his adventures was always a privilege which entailed discretion and reticence upon me. It is only appropriate that this long series of episodes should culminate in the most important international case which he has ever been called upon to handle.

It was July 1914 - the most terrible time in the history of the world. One might have thought already that God's curse hung heavy over a degenerate world, for there was an awesome hush and a feeling of vague expectancy in the sultry and stagnant air. That evening it was quite dark by the time I reached home. The sun had long set, but one blood-red gash like an open wound lay low in the distant west. Above, the stars were shining brightly, and below, the lights of the great city twinkled and glimmered on the winding river in the night. My companion's book and pipe lay by his chair, but he had disappeared. I looked about in the hope of seeing a note, but there was none.

The relations between us in those latter days were peculiar. He was a man of habits, narrow and concentrated habits, and I had become one of them. As an institution I was like the violin, the shag tobacco, the old black pipe, the index books, and others perhaps less excusable. When it was a case of active work and a comrade was needed upon whose nerve he could place some reliance, my role was obvious. But apart from this I had uses. I was a whetstone for his mind. I stimulated him. He liked to think aloud in my presence. His remarks could hardly be said to be made to me--many of them would have been as appropriately addressed to his bedstead--but none the less, having formed the habit, it had become in some way helpful that I should register and interject. If I irritated him by a certain methodical slowness in my mentality, that irritation served only to make his own flame-like intuitions and impressions flash up the more vividly and swiftly. Such was my humble role in our alliance.

"I suppose that Mr. Sherlock Holmes has gone out," I said to Mrs. Hudson as she came up to lower the blinds.

"No, sir. He has gone to his room, sir. Do you know, sir," sinking her voice into an impressive whisper, "I am afraid for his health!"

Mrs. Hudson, the landlady of Sherlock Holmes, was a long-suffering woman. Not only was her first-floor flat invaded at all hours by throngs of singular and often undesirable characters but her remarkable lodger showed an eccentricity and irregularity in his life which must have sorely tried her patience. His incredible untidiness, his addiction to music at strange hours, his occasional revolver practice within doors, his weird and often malodorous scientific experiments, and the atmosphere of violence and danger which hung around him made him the worst tenant in London. On the other hand, his payments were princely. I have no doubt that the house might have been purchased at the price which Holmes paid for his rooms during the years that I was with him.

The landlady stood in the deepest awe of him and never dared to interfere with him, however outrageous his proceedings might seem. She was fond of him, too, for he had a remarkable gentleness and courtesy in his dealings with women. He disliked and distrusted the sex, but he was always a chivalrous opponent. Knowing how genuine was her regard for him, I listened earnestly to her as she told me of the sad condition to which my poor friend was reduced.

"Well, he's that strange, sir. After you was gone he walked and he walked, up and down, and up and down, until I was weary of the sound of his footstep. Then I heard him talking to himself and muttering, and every time the bell rang out he came on the stairhead, with 'What is that, Mrs. Hudson?' And now he has slammed off to his room, but I can hear him walking away the same as ever. I hope he's not going to be ill, sir. I ventured to say something to him about cooling medicine, but he turned on me, sir, with such a look that I don't know how ever I got out of the room."

"I do not think that you have any cause to be uneasy, Mrs. Hudson," I answered. "I have seen him like this before. He has some small matter upon his mind which makes him restless. You know his way when he is keen on a case."

"Yes, sir, he is very hard at it just now. He gets paler and thinner, and he eats nothing. 'When will you be pleased to dine, Mr. Holmes?' I asked. 'Within the week,' he said."

I had tried to speak lightly to our worthy landlady, but I was myself somewhat uneasy when through the long night I still from time to time heard the dull sound of his tread, and knew how his keen spirit was chafing.

It was at a time Holmes's iron constitution again showed some symptoms of giving way in the face of constant hard work of a most exacting kind, aggravated, perhaps, by occasional indiscretions of his own. The state of his health was not a matter in which he himself took the faintest interest, for his mental detachment was absolute. One of the most remarkable characteristics of Sherlock Holmes was his power of throwing his brain out of action and switching all his thoughts on to lighter things whenever he had convinced himself that he could no longer work to advantage. All the more reason why his agitation made me uneasy.

I do not know how far Sherlock Holmes took any sleep that night, but when I came down to breakfast I found him pale and harassed, his bright eyes the brighter for the dark shadows round them. The carpet round his chair was littered with cigarette-ends. An open letter lay upon the table. My friend had no breakfast himself, for it was one of his peculiarities that in his more intense moments he would permit himself no food, and I have known him presume upon his iron strength until he has fainted from pure inanition. "At present I cannot spare energy and nerve force for digestion," he would say in answer to my medical remonstrances. I was not surprised, therefore, when this morning he left his meal untouched.

It was a blazing hot day. He was a late riser, as a rule, and Baker Street was like an oven. The glare of the sunlight upon the yellow brickwork of the house across the road was painful to the eye. It was hard to believe that these were the same walls which loomed so gloomily through the fogs of winter. Our blinds were half-drawn, and Holmes was reading and re-reading a letter which he had received by the morning post. For myself, my term of service in India had trained me to stand heat better than cold, and a thermometer at ninety was no hardship yet I yearned for the glades of the New Forest or the shingle of Southsea. A depleted bank account had caused me to postpone my holiday, and as to my companion, neither the country nor the sea presented the slightest attraction to him. He loved to lie in the very centre of five millions of people, with his filaments stretching out and running through them, responsive to every little rumour or suspicion of unsolved crime. Appreciation of nature found no place among his many gifts, and his only change was when he turned his mind from the evil-doer of the town to track down his brother of the country.

"I am inclined to think – " said I.

"I should do so," Sherlock Holmes remarked impatiently.

I believe that I am one of the most long-suffering of mortals; but I will admit that I was annoyed at the sardonic interruption. "Really, Holmes," said I severely, "you are a little trying at times."

He was too much absorbed with his own thoughts to give any immediate answer to my remonstrance. He leaned upon his hand, with his untasted breakfast before him, and he stared at the slip of paper which he had drawn from its envelope. Then he took the envelope itself, held it up to the light, and carefully studied both the exterior and the flap.

"There are one or two indications, and yet the utmost pains have been taken to remove all clues."

He was speaking to himself rather than to me; but my vexation disappeared in the interest which the words awakened.

"The address, you observe is printed in rough characters. Now, you would call it a guess, no doubt, but I am almost certain that this address has been written in a hotel."

"How in the world can you say that? We are coming now rather into the region of guesswork," said I.

"Say, rather, into the region where we balance probabilities and choose the most likely. It is the scientific use of the imagination, but we have always some material basis on which to start our speculation. If you examine it carefully you will see that both the pen and the ink have given the writer trouble. The pen has spluttered twice in a single word and has run dry three times in a short address, showing that there was little ink in the bottle. Now, a private pen or ink-bottle is seldom allowed to be in such a state, and the combination of the two must be quite rare. But you know the hotel ink and the hotel pen, where it is rare to get anything else.

"Halloa! Halloa! What's this? It is Petrovic's writing," said he thoughtfully. "I can hardly doubt that it is Petrovic's writing, though I have seen it only twice before. The Cyrillic e with the peculiar top flourish is distinctive. But if it is Petrovic, then it must be something of the very first importance."

"Who then is Petrovic?" I asked.

"Petrovic, Watson, is a nom-de-plume, a mere identification mark; but behind it lies a shifty and evasive personality. In a former letter he frankly informed me that the name was not his own, and defied me ever to trace him among the teeming millions of this great city. Petrovic is important, not for himself, but for the man with whom he is in touch. Picture to yourself the pilot fish with the shark, the jackal with the lion—anything that is insignificant in companionship with what is formidable: not only formidable, Watson, but sinister—in the highest degree sinister. That is where he comes within my purview. You have heard me speak of Colonel Dragutin Dimitrijević also known as Apis?"

"The leader of the group of Servian officers who brutally assassinated and then mutilated the bodies of the king and queen of Servia at Belgrade in 1903?"

"The very same."

"The infamous criminal, as notorious —"

"My blushes, Watson!" Holmes murmured in a deprecating voice.

"I was about to say, as he is unknown to the public."

"A touch! A distinct touch!" cried Holmes. "You are developing a certain unexpected vein of pawky humour, Watson, against which I must learn to guard myself. But in calling Dimitrijević a criminal you are uttering libel in the eyes of the law—and there lie the glory and the wonder of it! The greatest schemer since the death of Professor Moriarty, the organiser of every deviltry, the controlling brain of the underworld, a brain which may make or marr the destiny of nations—that's the man! But so aloof is he from general suspicion, so immune from criticism, so admirable in his management and self-effacement, that for those very words that you have uttered he could hale you to a court and emerge with your year's pension as a solatium for his wounded character. The Servian parliament described Dimitrijević as "the saviour of the fatherland" and he was appointed Professor of Tactics at their Military Academy. Is this a man to traduce? Foul-mouthed doctor and slandered Colonel—such would be your respective roles! That's genius, Watson. But if I am spared by lesser men, our day will surely come."

"May I be there to see!" I exclaimed devoutly. "But you were speaking of this man."

"Ah, yes—the so-called Petrovic is a link in the chain some little way from its great attachment. Petrovic is not quite a sound link—between ourselves. He is the only flaw in that chain so far as I have been able to test it."

"But no chain is stronger than its weakest link."

"Exactly, my dear Watson! Hence the extreme importance of Petrovic. Led on by some rudimentary aspirations towards right, and encouraged by the judicious stimulation of an occasional ten-pound note sent to him by devious methods, he has once or twice given me advance information which has been of value—that highest value which anticipates and prevents rather than avenges crime. I cannot doubt that, if we had the cipher, we should find that this communication is of the nature that I indicate."

Holmes flattened out the paper upon his unused plate. I rose and, leaning over him, stared down at the curious inscription, which ran as follows:

$$5.34 \quad C2 \quad 13 \quad 1 \quad 293 \quad 31 \quad 4 \quad \underline{10}$$

"What do you make of it, Holmes?"

"It is obviously an attempt to convey secret information."

"But what is the use of a cipher message without the cipher?"

"In this instance, none at all."

"Why do you say 'in this instance'?"

"Because there are many ciphers which I would read as easily as I do the apocrypha of the agony column: such crude devices amuse the intelligence without fatiguing it. But this is different. It is clearly a reference to the words in a page of some book. Until I am told which page and which book I am powerless."

"Then why has he not indicated the book?"

"Your native shrewdness, my dear Watson, that innate cunning which is the delight of your friends, would surely prevent you from inclosing cipher and message in the same envelope. Should it miscarry, you are undone. As it is, both have to go wrong before any harm comes from it. Our second post is now overdue, and I shall be surprised if it does not

15

bring us either a further letter of explanation, or, as is more probable, the very volume to which these figures refer."

Holmes's calculation was fulfilled within a few minutes by the appearance of Billy, the page, with the very letter which we were expecting.

"The same writing," remarked Holmes, as he opened the envelope, "and actually signed," he added in an exultant voice as he unfolded the epistle. "Come, we are getting on, Watson." His brow clouded, however, as he glanced over the contents.

"Dear me, this is disappointing! I fear, Watson, that all our expectations come to nothing. I trust that the man Petrovic will come to no harm."

DEAR MR. HOLMES [he says]:

"I will go no further in this matter. It is too dangerous—he suspects me. I can see that he suspects me. He came to me quite unexpectedly after I had actually addressed this envelope with the intention of sending you the key to the cipher. I was able to cover it up. If he had seen it, it would have gone hard with me. But I read suspicion in his eyes. Please burn the cipher message, which can now be of no use to you.

"Petrovic."

Holmes sat for some little time twisting this letter between his fingers, and frowning, as he stared into the distance.

"After all," he said at last, "there may be nothing in it. It may be only his guilty conscience. Knowing himself to be a traitor, he may have read the accusation in the other's eyes."

"The other being, I presume, Apis."

"No less! When any of that party talk about 'He' you know whom they mean. There is one predominant 'He' for all of them."

"But what can he do?"

"Hum! That is a large question. When you have one of the first brains of Europe up against you, and all the powers of darkness at his back, there are infinite possibilities. Anyhow, Friend Petrovic is evidently scared out of his senses—kindly compare the writing in the note to that upon its envelope; which was done, he tells us, before this ill-omened visit. The one is clear and firm. The other hardly legible."

"Why did he write at all? Why did he not simply drop it?"

"Because he feared I would make some inquiry after him in that case, and possibly bring trouble on him."

"No doubt," said I. "Of course." I had picked up the original cipher message and was bending my brows over it. "It is maddening to think that an important secret may lie here on this slip of paper, and that it is beyond human power to penetrate it."

Sherlock Holmes had pushed away his untasted breakfast and lit the unsavoury pipe which was the companion of his deepest meditations. "I wonder!" said he, leaning back and staring at the ceiling. "Perhaps there are points which have escaped your Machiavellian intellect. Let us consider the problem in the light of pure reason. This man's reference is to a book. That is our point of departure."

"A somewhat vague one."

"Let us see then if we can narrow it down. As I focus my mind upon it, it seems rather less impenetrable. What indications have we as to this book?"

"None."

"Well, well, it is surely not quite so bad as that. The cipher message begins with a large 534, does it not? We may take it as a working hypothesis that 534 is the particular page to which the cipher refers. So our book has already become a LARGE book, which is surely something gained. What other indications have we as to the nature of this large book? The next sign is C2. What do you make of that, Watson?"

"Chapter the second, no doubt."

"Hardly that, Watson. You will, I am sure, agree with me that if the page be given, the number of the chapter is immaterial. Also that if page 534 finds us only in the second chapter, the length of the first one must have been really intolerable."

"Column!" I cried.

"Brilliant, Watson. You are scintillating this morning. If it is not column, then I am very much deceived. So now, you see, we begin to visualize a large book printed in double columns which are each of a considerable length, since one of the words is numbered in the document as the two hundred and ninety-third. Have we reached the limits of what reason can supply?"

"I fear that we have."

"Surely you do yourself an injustice. One more coruscation, my dear Watson—yet another brain-wave! Had the volume been an unusual one, he would have sent it to me.

Instead of that, he had intended, before his plans were nipped, to send me the clue in this envelope. He says so in his note. This would seem to indicate that the book is one which he thought I would have no difficulty in finding for myself. He had it—and he imagined that I would have it, too. In short, Watson, it is a very common book."

"What you say certainly sounds plausible."

"So we have contracted our field of search to a large book, printed in double columns and in common use."

"The Bible!" I cried triumphantly.

"Good, Watson, good! But not, if I may say so, quite good enough! Even if I accepted the compliment for myself I could hardly name any volume which would be less likely to lie at the elbow of one of Apis' associates. Besides, the editions of Holy Writ are so numerous that he could hardly suppose that two copies would have the same pagination. This is clearly a book which is standardised. He knows for certain that his page 534 will exactly agree with my page 534."

"But very few books would correspond with that."

"Exactly. Therein lies our salvation. Our search is narrowed down to standardised books which anyone may be supposed to possess."

"Bradshaw!"

"There are difficulties, Watson. The vocabulary of Bradshaw is nervous and terse, but limited. The selection of words would hardly lend itself to the sending of general messages. We will eliminate Bradshaw. The dictionary is, I fear, inadmissible for the same reason. What then is left?"

"An almanac!"

"Excellent, Watson! I am very much mistaken if you have not touched the spot. An almanac! Let us consider the claims of Whitaker's Almanac. It is in common use. It has the requisite number of pages. It is in double column. Though reserved in its earlier vocabulary, it becomes, if I remember right, quite garrulous towards the end." He picked the volume from his desk. "Here is page 534, column two, a substantial block of print dealing, I perceive, with the trade and resources of British India. Jot down the words, Watson! Number thirteen is 'Mahratta.' Not, I fear, a very auspicious beginning. Number one is 'Government'; which at least makes sense, though the Mahratta government is somewhat irrelevant to ourselves, Apis and the Black Hand. Now let us try again. What does the Mahratta government do? Alas! the next word is 'pig's-bristles.' We are undone, my good Watson! It is finished!"

He had spoken in jesting vein, but the twitching of his bushy eyebrows bespoke his disappointment and irritation. I sat helpless and unhappy. A long silence was broken by a sudden exclamation from Holmes, who dashed at a cupboard, from which he emerged with a second yellow-covered volume in his hand.

"We pay the price, Watson, for being too up-to-date!" he cried. "We are before our time, and suffer the usual penalties. Being more methodical, we have properly laid in the new almanac. It is possible that Petrovic took his message from the old one. No doubt he would have told us so had his letter of explanation been written. Now let us see what page 534 has in store for us. Number thirteen is 'watch,' which is much more promising. Number one is 'the'—'Watch the' — Holmes's eyes were gleaming with excitement, and his thin, nervous fingers twitched as he counted the words—"gold. Ha! Ha! Capital! Put that down, Watson. 'Watch the gold—in—number—could.' We were good till the last."

"But the last, the number 10, is underlined like no other."

"Correct again Watson! Brilliant. It is meant itself as the number 10. 'Watch the gold in number 10.' There, Watson! What do you think of pure reason and its fruit? If the green-grocer had such a thing as a laurel wreath, I should send Billy round for it."

Sherlock Holmes closed his eyes and placed his elbows upon the arms of his chair, with his finger-tips together. "The ideal reasoner," he remarked, "would, when he had once been shown a single fact in all its bearings, deduce from it not only all the chain of events which led up to it but also all the results which would follow from it. As Cuvier could correctly describe a whole animal by the contemplation of a single bone, so the observer who has thoroughly understood one link in a series of incidents should be able to accurately state all the other ones, both before and after. We have not yet grasped the results which the reason alone can attain to. Problems may be solved in the study which have baffled all those who have sought a solution by the aid of their senses. To carry the art, however, to its highest pitch, it is necessary that the reasoner should be able to utilise all the facts which have come to his knowledge; and this in itself implies, as you will readily see, a possession of all knowledge, which, even in these days of free education and encyclopaedias, is a somewhat rare accomplishment. It is not so impossible, however, that a man should possess all knowledge which is likely to be useful to him in his work, and this I have endeavoured in my case to do. If I remember rightly, you on one occasion, in the early days of our friendship, defined my limits in a very precise fashion."

"Yes," I answered, laughing. "It was a singular document. Philosophy, astronomy, and politics were marked at zero, I remember. Botany variable, geology profound as regards the mud-stains from any region within fifty miles of town, chemistry eccentric, anatomy unsystematic, sensational literature and crime records unique, violin-player, boxer, swordsman, lawyer, and self-poisoner by cocaine and tobacco. Those, I think, were the main points of my analysis."

Holmes grinned at the last item. "Well," he said, "I say now, as I said then, that a man should keep his little brain-attic stocked with all the furniture that he is likely to use, and the rest he can put away in the lumber-room of his library, where he can get it if he wants it. Now, for such a case as the one which has been submitted to us, we need certainly to muster all our resources."

I was staring at the strange message which I had scrawled, as he deciphered it, upon a sheet of foolscap on my knee.

"What a queer, scrambling way of expressing his meaning!" said I.

"On the contrary, he has done quite remarkably well," said Holmes. "When you search a single column for words with which to express your meaning, you can hardly expect to get everything you want. You are bound to leave something to the intelligence of your correspondent. The purport is perfectly clear. Some deviltry is intended against the gold at number 10. There is our result—and a very workmanlike little bit of analysis it was!"

"But Holmes, it still means nothing to me. What gold is there at what number 10?"

"It can only refer to 10 Downing Street, Watson, the headquarters of the British Government and the official residence and office of the First Lord of the Treasury. It is where our gold reserves are stored. There is little we can do about it just now. However, I will make some inquiries."

Holmes had the impersonal joy of the true artist in his better work, even as he mourned darkly when it fell below the high level to which he aspired. He was still chuckling over his success when the door swung open into the room.

"By Jove! Here comes something else to break our dead monotony."

It was the maid with a telegram this time. Holmes tore it open and burst out laughing.

"Well, well! What next?" said he. "Brother Mycroft is coming round."

"Why not?" I asked.

"Why not? It is as if you met a tram-car coming down a country lane. Mycroft as you know has his rails and he runs on them. His Pall Mall lodgings, the Diogenes Club, Whitehall--that is his cycle. He has an extraordinary faculty for figures, and audits the books in some of the government departments. Mycroft lodges in Pall Mall, and he walks round the corner into Whitehall every morning and back every evening. From year's end to year's end he takes no other exercise, and is seen nowhere else, except only in the Diogenes Club, which is just opposite his rooms. Only twice has he been here, you will recall. What upheaval can possibly have derailed him this time?"

"Does he not explain?"

Holmes handed me his brother's telegram.

Must see you over Wilson. Coming at once.

MYCROFT

"What on earth can it mean? Who is Wilson, and what is he to Mycroft?" mused Holmes out loud.

"I have it," I cried, and plunged among the litter of morning papers I had left upon the sofa. "Yes, yes, here he is, sure enough!" I read aloud, "At around midnight yesterday, Field-Marshal Henry Wilson was found dead on the steps leading up to his front door."

Holmes sat up at attention, his pipe halfway to his lips.

"This must be serious, Watson. A death which has caused my brother to alter his habits can be no ordinary one. A distinguished soldier. Behold the link with Brother Mycroft! That Mycroft should break out in this erratic fashion! A planet might as well leave its orbit. By the way, do you recall his last visit?"

I had, of course, some recollection of the Adventures of the Greek Interpreter and of the Bruce Partington Plans.

"You at first told me that Mycroft had some small office under the British government."

Holmes chuckled.

"I did not know you quite so well in those days. One has to be discreet when one talks of high matters of state. You were right in thinking that he was under the British government. I was also right in a sense when I said that occasionally he IS the British government. Mycroft draws four hundred and fifty pounds a year, remains a subordinate, has no ambitions of any kind, will receive neither honour nor title, and remains the most indispensable man in the country."

"Well, his position is assuredly unique."

"He has made it for himself. There has never been anything like it before, nor will be again. As you may have observed, he has the tidiest and most orderly brain, with the greatest capacity for storing facts, of any man living. He is my superior in observation and deduction. If the art of the detective began and ended in reasoning from an arm-chair, my brother would be the greatest criminal agent that ever lived. But he has no ambition and no energy. What is to me a means of livelihood is to him the merest hobby of a dilettante. He will not even go out of his way to verify his own solutions, and would rather be considered wrong than take the trouble to prove himself right. Again and again I have taken a problem to him, and have received an explanation which has afterwards proved to be the correct one. And yet he was absolutely incapable of working out the practical points which must be gone into before a case could be laid before a judge or jury. The same great powers which I have turned to the detection of crime he has used for his particular business. The conclusions of every department are passed to him, and he is the central exchange, the clearinghouse, which makes out the balance. All other men are specialists, but his specialism is omniscience. We will suppose that a minister needs information as to a point which involves the Navy, Belgium, France, Austria-Hungary and the bimetallic question; he could get his separate advices from various departments upon each, but only Mycroft can focus them all, and say offhand how each factor would affect the other. They began by using him as a short-cut, a convenience; now he has made himself an essential. In that great brain of his everything is pigeon-holed and can be handed out in an instant. Again and again his word has decided the national policy. He lives in it. He thinks of nothing else save when, as an intellectual exercise, he unbends if I call upon him and ask him to advise me on one of my little problems. But Jupiter is descending to-day. What on earth can it mean?"

"No data yet," I answered. "I have heard you say, 'It is a capital mistake to theorize before you have all the evidence. It biases the judgment.'"

"Good!" said Holmes. "Excellent! Really, Watson, you excel yourself," said he, pushing back his chair and lighting a cigarette. "I am bound to say that in all the accounts which you have been so good as to give of my own small achievements you have habitually underrated your own abilities. It may be that you are not yourself luminous, but you are a conductor of light. Some people without possessing genius have a remarkable power of stimulating it."

Chapter 2 - Mycroft states the case

There was some talking in gruff voices outside, and Mrs. Hudson opened the door to say that there were three men inquiring for Mr. Holmes.

A moment later the tall and portly form of Mycroft Holmes was ushered into the room. Heavily built and massive, there was a suggestion of uncouth physical inertia in the figure, but above this unwieldy frame there was perched a head so masterful in its brow, so alert in its steel-grey, deep-set eyes, so firm in its lips, and so subtle in its play of expression, that after the first glance one forgot the gross body and remembered only the dominant mind.

At his heels we found two visitors of European fame now within the walls of our humble room in Baker Street. The one, dark, clear-cut, and elegant, hardly yet of middle age, and endowed with every beauty of body and of mind, was none other than the illustrious Sir Edward Grey, Foreign Secretary. The other, austere, high-nosed, eagle-eyed, and dominant, was David Lloyd George, Chancellor of the Exchequer, and the most rising statesman in the country. They sat side by side upon our paper-littered settee, and it was easy to see from their worn and anxious faces that it was business of the most pressing importance which had brought them. The Foreign Secretary's thin, blue-veined hands were clasped tightly over the ivory head of his umbrella, and his gaunt, ascetic face looked gloomily from Holmes to me. The Chancellor pulled nervously at his moustache and fidgeted with the seals of his watch-chain.

Mycroft Holmes subsided into an armchair.

"You had my note, Sherlock?"

"Yes, but it explained nothing."

"It was too delicate a thing for me to put the

details on paper. And too complicated. It was only face to face I could do it."

"Well, we are at your disposal."

"A most annoying business, Sherlock. I extremely dislike altering my habits, but the powers that be would take no denial. In the present state of the world it is most awkward that I should be away from the office. But it is a real crisis. I have never seen Prime Minister Asquith so upset. As to the Admiralty--it is buzzing like an overturned bee-hive. Churchill is bellicose."

"Well, well, you must not do anything rash, or that you might repent. Let me hear all about it. Give me the facts."

"You are of course aware of the unfortunate assassination of Archduke Franz Ferdinand, heir to the Austro-Hungarian throne and his morganatic wife, in Sarajevo on 28 June, St. Vitus's Day or *Vidov Dan* as it is known there," began Mycroft.

"Yes, we have seen the papers. An unfortunately provocative day to have chosen," said Sherlock Holmes.

"Austria's annexation of Bosnia-Herzegovina in the midst of Servian hatred and Russian resentment is a ticking diplomatic time bomb that could go off at any time and Ferdinand's death may set in train a series of events that could culminated in war. Austria-Hungary's reaction to the death of their heir is, as yet, unclear, but it is likely to be provocative. Amid the action and reaction of so dense a swarm of activity and intrigue, every possible combination of events may be expected to take place. I am conscious myself of a weight at my heart and a feeling of impending danger—ever present danger, which is the more terrible because I am unable to define it. It is likely that the Servian government will be implicated in the machinations and that the Black Hand is responsible. If the Austrians opt to take this opportunity to 'solve the Servian question once and for all', as Conrad is so fond of iterating, thus crushing the nationalist movement there and cementing Austria's influence in the Balkans, I fear the effects may be catastrophic."

"You are certainly a model client Mycroft. You have the correct intuition. We were just discussing Apis as I had a letter from one of his henchmen. Let us see, now," said Holmes, "Make a long arm, Watson, and see what B has to say."

I leaned back and took down the great index volume to which he referred. For many years he had adopted a system of docketing all paragraphs concerning men and things, so that it was difficult to name a subject or a person on which he could not at once furnish information. Holmes balanced it on his knee, and his eyes moved slowly and lovingly over the record of old cases, mixed with the accumulated information of a lifetime.

"What have we here? The Black Hand. Yes, a dangerous organisation—so dangerous that even the most saintly dare only whisper their opinions with bated breath, lest something which fell from their lips might be misconstrued, and bring down a swift retribution upon them. It is led by Colonel Dragutin Dimitrijević, also known as Apis, who is the chief of the Intelligence Department of the Servian General Staff. Other prominent members are Antonije Antić, Dragutin Dulić, Milan Marinković, and Nikodije Popović; all members of the Servian Army. The group is mainly made up of junior army officers but also includes lawyers, journalists and university professors."

"A singular group of people," commented Mycroft.

"The Black Hand. This terrible secret society was originally formed as 'National Defence' in 1908 by Servian soldiers after the annexation of Bosnia and Herzegovina by Austria. It officially began as 'The Black Hand', a name derived from the Servian meaning 'Unification or Death' in

May 1911 and it rapidly formed local branches in different areas, notably in Belgrade, Slovenia, Bosnia, Herzegovina, and Istria. It is known to have hundreds, if not thousands of members. Its power is used for political purposes, principally for the creation of a Greater Servia and driving from the region those who are opposed to its views. Its outrages are usually preceded by a warning sent to the marked man in some fantastic but generally recognised shape—a stylised cross or a clenched fist holding a skull and cross-bones. On receiving this the victim might either openly abjure his former ways, or might fly from the country. If he braved the matter out, death would unfailingly come upon him, and usually in some strange and unforeseen manner. So perfect was the organisation of the society, and so systematic its methods, that there is hardly a case upon record where any man succeeded in braving it with impunity, or in which any of its outrages were traced home to the perpetrators. For some years the organisation has flourished in spite of the efforts of the Austrian government."

"Formidable opponents indeed," I ventured.

Sherlock Holmes continued, "Not the Inquisition of Seville, nor the German Vehm-gericht, nor the Secret Societies of Italy or the State of Utah, were ever able to put a more formidable machinery in motion than that which cast a cloud over the Balkan States. Its invisibility, and the mystery which is attached to it, makes this organisation doubly terrible. Its stated means are violence and it appears to be omniscient and omnipotent, and yet it is neither seen nor heard. The man who holds out against it vanishes away, and none know whither he has gone or what has befallen him. His wife and his children await him at home, but no father ever returns to tell them how he had fared at the hands of his secret judges. A rash word or a hasty act is followed by annihilation, and yet none know what the nature might be of this terrible power which is suspended over them. No wonder that men go about in fear and trembling, and that even in the heart of the city they dare not whisper the doubts which oppress them."

"Well done Sherlock. You are well-informed as usual," said Mycroft. "I know you care nothing about politics Sherlock, but I expect you are aware there was a declaration made in 1904 between the United Kingdom and France respecting Egypt and Morocco. What you do not know is that there is also a secret part to this treaty, this entente, which is related to the movements of the British Expeditionary Force and our cooperation with the French in the event of a war. Its importance can hardly be exaggerated. Without going into details, I may say that it defines the position of Great Britain towards the Triple Alliance, and fore-shadows the policy which this country would pursue in the event of the Germans invading France or Belgium or their fleet gaining ascendancy in the Mediterranean. At the end are the signatures of the high dignitaries who have signed it. That is a State secret of the utmost importance. And it is the secret articles—which may well mean the expenditure of a thousand millions and the lives of a hundred thousand men—which have become lost in an unaccountable fashion."

"This," said Sir Edward, taking out a grey roll of paper, "is the original of the treaty between England and France of which, I regret to say, some rumours have already got into the public press. It is of enormous importance that nothing should leak out regarding the secret articles. The Germans or the Russian embassy would pay an immense sum to learn the contents of the treaty."

"But you have recovered the document?"

"Ah, there's the point! We have not. Fortunately, it has not come out. The press would be furious if it did. The full document, the nine public articles and the five secret articles, was taken from Woolwich. Only the public parts were found in the pocket of Wilson after he was murdered. The secret parts are gone--stolen, vanished."

"In whose interest is it that the treaty should come out? Why should anyone desire to steal it or to publish it?"

"There you take me into regions of high international politics," answered Mycroft. "But if you consider the European situation you will have no difficulty in perceiving the motive. The whole of Europe is an armed camp. There is a double league which makes a fair balance of military power. Great Britain holds the scales. If Britain were driven into war with one confederacy, it would assure supremacy over the other confederacy."

"It is then in the interest of our enemies to secure and publish this treaty, so as to make a breach between some country and ours?"

"Yes, sir," agreed Sir Edward.

"And to whom would this document be sent if it fell into the hands of an enemy?"

"To any of the great Chancelleries of Europe. It is probably speeding on its way thither at the present instant as fast as steam can take it. It has been the most jealously guarded of all government secrets and if it gets out to Russia or Germany it could make an already inflamed situation even worse."

Sir Edward dropped his head on his chest and groaned aloud. The Chancellor placed his hand kindly upon his shoulder.

"It is your misfortune, my dear fellow. No one can blame you. There is no precaution which you have neglected," said the Chancellor.

Mycroft continued, "Because the document in question is of such immense importance that its publication might very easily—I might almost say probably—lead to European complications of the utmost moment. Given the assassination of the Archduke and the state of European affairs at the moment, it is not too much to say that peace or war may hang upon the issue. Unless its recovery can be attended with the utmost secrecy, then it may as well not be recovered at all, for all that is aimed at by those who have taken it is that its contents should be generally known."

"I understand." said Sherlock Holmes. "Have you lost any documents before?"

"No, sir."

"Who is there in England who did know of the existence of this secret treaty?"

"Each member of the Cabinet was informed, but the pledge of secrecy which attends every Cabinet meeting was increased by the solemn warning which was given by the Prime Minister." His handsome face was distorted with a spasm of despair, and his hands tore at his hair. For a moment we caught a glimpse of the natural man, impulsive, ardent, keenly sensitive. The next the aristocratic mask was replaced, and the gentle voice had returned. "Besides the members of the Cabinet there are two, or possibly three, senior departmental officials, and Wilson of course, who knew of the secret articles. No one else in England, Mr. Holmes, I assure you."

"But abroad?"

"I believe that no one abroad has seen it save the Frenchmen who were involved in writing it, Loubet and Poincaré, and I am well convinced that their Ministers—that the usual official channels have not been employed."

Holmes considered for some little time. "Now, I should be much obliged if you would tell me exactly the circumstances under which this document disappeared," said Sherlock Holmes.

"Every effort has been made to keep the secret. The treaty, which is exceedingly intricate, comprising some fourteen separate agreements, nine public and five secret, each essential to the working of the whole, is kept in an elaborate safe in a confidential office adjoining the arsenal, with burglar-proof doors and windows. Under no conceivable circumstances was the treaty to be taken from the office. If the Prime Minister desired to consult the document, even he was forced to go to the Woolwich office for the purpose. And yet here we find it in the pocket of Wilson after being murdered in the heart of London. From an official point of view it's simply awful.

"We also know several other things, and there are more reasons we have come to you. It is clear to us that the Germans are stirring up trouble in Ireland to keep us looking to home-shores. We think they may actually be behind the murder of Wilson, and we think there is a plot to steal ... to try to steal, the gold in our vaults."

"It is our French gold," whispered David Lloyd George, Chancellor of the Exchequer. "We have had several warnings that an attempt might be made upon it."

"Our French gold?"

"Yes. We had occasion some months ago to strengthen our resources, lest we resort to printing paper money, and borrowed for that purpose 3,000,000 napoleons from the Bank of France. It has become known that we have never had occasion to unpack the money, and that it is still lying in our vaults in the basement of Number 10. Our reserve of bullion is much larger at present than is usually kept, and many have expressed misgivings upon the subject."

Sherlock Holmes remained silent for some little time with his brows knitted. It was obviously his intention to say nothing of the cypher message. I knew my friend's plans would gradually reveal themselves. There was a curious secretive streak in the man which led to many dramatic effects, but left even his closest friend guessing as to what his exact plans might be. He pushed to an extreme the axiom that the only safe plotter was he who plotted alone. I was nearer him than anyone else, and yet I was always conscious of the gap between.

Mycroft continued, "We suspect the Germans are looking to steal the Gold to fund their efforts and, since it is French Gold on loan to us, if it goes missing, it may help to upset the secret *entente* which they suspect between England and France. You must drop everything, Sherlock. Never mind your usual petty puzzles of the police-court. These are vital international problems that you have to solve. Why did Wilson have the treaty, where are the missing parts, how can we keep our Gold safe, how can these evils be set right? Find an answer to all these questions and you will have done good service for your country."

"Why do you not solve it yourself, Mycroft? You can see as far as I."

"Possibly, Sherlock. But it is a question of getting details. Give me your details, and from an armchair I will return you an excellent expert opinion. But to run here and run there, to cross-question witnesses, and lie on my face with a lens to my eye--it is not my metier. No, you are the one man who can clear these matters up. If you have a fancy to see your name in the next honours list--"

My friend smiled and shook his head.

"I play the game for the game's own sake," said he. "But the problems certainly present some points of interest, and I shall be very pleased to look into them. Some more facts, please."

"I have jotted down the more essential ones upon this sheet of paper, together with a few addresses which you will find of service. First the treaty. The actual official guardian of the treaty is the famous government expert, Sir James Walter, whose decorations and sub-titles fill two lines of a book of reference. He has grown grey in the service, is a gentleman, a favoured guest in the most exalted houses, and, above all, a man whose patriotism is beyond suspicion. He is one of two who have a key to the safe. I may add that the treaty was undoubtedly in the office during working hours on Monday, and that Sir James left for London about three o'clock taking his key with him. He was at the house of Admiral Sinclair at Barclay Square during the whole of the evening when this incident occurred."

"Has the fact been verified?"

"Yes; the senior clerk, Mr. Sidney Johnson, has testified to his departure from Woolwich, and Admiral Sinclair to his arrival in London; so Sir James is no longer a direct factor in the problem."

"Who was the other man with a key?"

"The senior clerk, Mr. Sidney Johnson. He is a man of forty, married, with five children. He is a silent, morose man, but he has, on the whole, an excellent record in the public service. He is unpopular with his colleagues, but a hard worker. According to his own account, corroborated only by the word of his wife, he was at home the whole of Monday evening after office hours, and his key has never left the watch-chain upon which it hangs."

"Tell us about Wilson."

"He has been more than thirty years in the service. Henry Hughes Wilson, 1st Baronet was one of our most senior Army staff officers and was briefly an Irish Unionist politician. Wilson served as Commandant of the Staff College, Camberley, and then as Director of Military Operations at the War Office, in which post he played a vital role in drawing up plans to deploy an Expeditionary Force to France in the event of war, a policy not favoured by all in the

Cabinet I may add. Wilson, in other words, was the architect of our current military strategy and of these secret plans. A flamboyant personage and an eloquent speaker on behalf of Anglo-Irish Unionism. He evoked the hatred of his nationalist countrymen, and it is they who are suspected of his murder yesterday on his door-steps."

"Yes, we also saw that in the papers this morning," said Sherlock Holmes. "Who locked up the treaty Monday night?"

"Mr. Sidney Johnson, the senior clerk."

"Well, it is surely perfectly clear who took them away. They were actually found upon the person of Wilson after he was murdered. That seems final, does it not?"

"It does, Sherlock, and yet it leaves so much unexplained. In the first place, why did he take them?"

"I presume they were of value?"

"He could have got several thousands for them very easily."

"Can you suggest any possible motive for taking the papers except to sell them?"

"No, I cannot."

"Then we must take that as our working hypothesis. Wilson took the papers. Now this could only be done by having a false key--"

"Several false keys. He had to open the building and the room."

"He had, then, several false keys. He took the papers to sell them. While on this treasonable mission he met his end."

"No better explanation can be given with our present knowledge; and yet consider, Sherlock, how much you leave untouched. We will suppose, for argument's sake, that Wilson had determined to convey these papers to London for sale. He would naturally have made an appointment with the foreign agent that evening and returned the papers. He must bring

37

back the papers before morning or the loss may be discovered. Instead of that he carried them around with him on Tuesday and then is suddenly murdered on his way home. He took away the whole. Only the public articles were found in his pocket. What has become of the others? He certainly would not leave them of his own free will. Then, again, where is the price of his treason? One would have expected to find a large sum of money in his pocket or his home and none was found."

Holmes shook his head mournfully.

"You think, sir, that unless this document is recovered there will be war?"

"I think it is very probable," said the Foreign Secretary.

"Then, sir, prepare for war."

"That is a hard saying, Mr. Holmes."

"Consider the facts, sir. It is inconceivable that the treaty was taken before the end of working hours on Monday, since I understand that several people were in the office until closing. It was taken, then, Monday evening. Now, sir, if a document of this importance were taken at that time, where can it be now? No one has any reason to retain it. It has been passed rapidly on to those who need it. What chance have we now to overtake or even to trace it? It is beyond our reach."

The Foreign Secretary rose from the settee.

"What you say is perfectly logical, Mr. Holmes. I feel that the matter is indeed out of our hands."

"Let us presume, for argument's sake, that the document was taken by Wilson—"

"But he is an old, trusted and tried servant of the Crown."

"I understand you, yet it must, then, be somebody who has taken it. To whom would the thief take it? To one of several international spies and secret agents, whose names are tolerably familiar to me. The theory holds together. But if this is true, then the case is at an end. On the one hand, the traitor is dead. On the other, the secret treaty is presumably already on the Continent. What is there for us to do?"

"To act, Sherlock--to act!" cried Mycroft, springing to his feet. "All my instincts are against this explanation. Use your powers! Go to the scene of the crime! See the people concerned! Leave no stone unturned! In all your career you have never had so great a chance of serving your country."

"There are three agents who may be said to be the heads of their profession. I will begin my research by going round and finding if each of them is at his post. If one is missing—especially if he has disappeared recently—we will have some indication as to where the document has gone."

"Why should he be missing?" asked the Foreign Secretary. "He would take the letter to an Embassy in London, as likely as not."

"I fancy not. These agents work independently, and their relations with the Embassies are often strained."

The Foreign Secretary nodded his acquiescence.

"I believe you are right, Sherlock. He would take so valuable a prize to headquarters with his own hands. I think that your course of action is an excellent one," said Mycroft. "Now, as to the gold reserves ..."

"Let us leave the question of the gold. I have one or two inquiries I can make on that account and in the meantime we can only concentrate our attention upon the missing treaty. It is of the highest importance in the art of detection to be able to recognise, out of a number of facts, which are incidental and which vital. Otherwise your energy and attention must be dissipated instead of being concentrated. Now, in this case there is not the slightest doubt in my mind that the key of the whole matter must be the missing document. Once that is addressed, we can turn our attention to the gold."

"Well, you are master of the situation. Meanwhile, we cannot neglect all our other duties on account of this misfortune, however grievous. Should there be any fresh developments during the day we shall communicate with you, and you will no doubt let us know the results of your own inquiries."

"Good-bye, Gentlemen. I shall let you have a report every evening, but I warn you in advance that you have little to expect."

The two statesmen bowed and walked gravely from the room with Mycroft following.

When our illustrious visitors had departed Holmes lit his pipe in silence and sat for some time lost in the deepest thought. "A chaotic case, my dear Watson," said Holmes. "It will not be possible for you to present in that compact form which is dear to your heart. It concerns two problems, one murder, several groups of mysterious persons, and is further complicated by the highly respectable presence of our Ministerial visitors, our friend Petrovic, and Apis, whose inclusion shows me that the situation is serious. It is remarkable not only for the fact that amid a perfect jungle of possibilities we, with our worthy collaborator, Petrovic, whose warning we have kept a close hold on, may help guide us along the crooked."

"This is all very well," said I, "but the thing becomes more unintelligible than ever. What are you going to do?" I asked.

"To smoke," he answered. "It is quite a three pipe problem, and I beg that you will not speak to me for fifty minutes." He curled himself up in his chair, with his thin knees drawn up to his hawk-like nose, and there he sat with his eyes closed and his black clay pipe thrusting out like the bill of some strange bird.

I had reopened the morning papers and was immersed in a sensational crime which had occurred in London the night before, when my friend gave an exclamation, sprang to his feet with the gesture of a man who has made up his mind, and laid his pipe down upon the mantelpiece.

"Yes," said he, "there is no better way of approaching it. The situation is desperate, but not hopeless. Even now, if we could be sure which of them has taken it, it is just possible that it has not yet passed out of his hands. After all, it is a question of money with these fellows, and I have the British treasury behind me. If it is on the market I will buy it—if it means another penny on the income-tax. It is conceivable that the fellow might hold it back to see what bids come from this side before he tries his luck on the other. There are only those three capable of playing so bold a game—there are Oberstein, La Rothiere, and James Larrabee. I will see each of them."

I glanced at my morning paper.

"Is that James Larrabee of Godolphin Street?"

"Yes."

"You will not see him."

"Why not?"

"He was murdered in his house last night."

My friend has so often astonished me in the course of our adventures that it was with a sense of exultation that I realised how completely I had astonished him. He stared in amazement, and then snatched the paper from my hands. This was the paragraph which I had been engaged in reading when he rose from his chair.

MURDER IN WESTMINSTER

A crime of mysterious character was committed last night at 16 Godolphin Street, one of the old-fashioned and secluded rows of eighteenth century houses which lie between the river and the Abbey, almost in the shadow of the great Tower of the Houses of Parliament. This small but select mansion has been inhabited for some years by Mr. James Larrabee, well known in society circles both on account of his charming personality and because he has the well-deserved reputation of being one of the best amateur tenors in the country. Mr. Larrabee is an unmarried man, thirty-four years of age, and his establishment consists of Mrs. Pringle, an elderly housekeeper, and of Mitton, his valet. The former retires early and sleeps at the top of the house. The valet was out for the evening, visiting a friend at Hammersmith. From ten o'clock onward Mr. Larrabee had the house to himself. What occurred during that time has not yet transpired, but at a quarter to twelve Police-constable Barrett, passing along Godolphin Street observed that the door of No. 16 was ajar. He knocked, but received no answer. Perceiving a light in the front room, he advanced into the passage and again knocked, but without reply. He then pushed open the door and entered. The room was in a state of wild disorder, the furniture being all swept to one side, and one chair lying on its back in the centre. Beside this chair, and still grasping one of its legs, lay the unfortunate tenant of the house. He had been stabbed to the heart and must have died instantly. The knife with which the crime had been committed was a curved Indian dagger, plucked down from a trophy of Oriental arms which adorned one of the walls. Robbery does not appear to have been the motive of the crime, for there had been no attempt to remove the valuable contents of the room. Mr. James Larrabee was so well known and popular that his violent and mysterious fate will arouse painful interest and intense sympathy in a widespread circle of friends.

"Well, Watson, what do you make of this?" asked Holmes, after a long pause.

"It is an amazing coincidence."

"A coincidence! Here is one of the three men whom we had named as possible actors in this drama, and he meets a violent death during the very hours when we know that that drama was being enacted. The odds are enormous against its being coincidence. No figures could express them. No, my dear Watson, the two events are connected—MUST be connected. It is for us to find the connection."

"But now the official police must know all."

"Not at all. They know all they see at Godolphin Street. They know—and shall know—nothing of the missing parts of the treaty. Only WE know of both events, and can trace the relation between them."

Chapter 3: The missing treaty

"We certainly owe Brother Mycroft a debt for having introduced us to what promises to be a really very remarkable case."

His eager face still wore that expression of intense and high-strung energy, which showed me that some novel and suggestive circumstance had opened up a stimulating line of thought. See the foxhound with hanging ears and drooping tail as it lolls about the kennels, and compare it with the same hound as, with gleaming eyes and straining muscles, it runs upon a breast-high scent--such was the change in Holmes since the morning. He was a different man from the figure in the mouse-coloured dressing-gown who had prowled so restlessly only a few hours before round the room.

"There is material here. There is scope," said he. "I am dull indeed not to have understood its possibilities."

"Even now they are dark to me."

"We have quite a little round of afternoon calls to make," said he. "I think that Sir James Walter claims our first attention."

I assented gladly, and we descended together. We stepped calmly into a cab, the driver, whipped up the horse, and brought us in a short time to our destination. The house of the famous official was a fine villa with green lawns stretching down to the Thames. A butler answered our ring.

"Sir James, sir!" said he with solemn face. "Sir James died this morning."

"Good heavens!" cried Holmes in amazement. "How did he die?"

"Perhaps you would care to step in, sir, and see his brother, Colonel Valentine?"

"Yes, we had best do so."

We were ushered into a dim-lit drawing-room, where an instant later we were joined by a tall, handsome, light-beared man of fifty, the younger brother of the dead Sir James. His wild eyes, stained cheeks, and unkempt hair all spoke of the sudden blow which had fallen upon the household. He was hardly articulate as he spoke of it.

"It was this horrible scandal," said he. "My brother, Sir James, was a man of sensitive honour, and he could not survive such an affair. It broke his heart. He was always so proud of the efficiency of his department, and this was a crushing blow."

"We had hoped that he might have given us some indications which would have helped us to clear the matter up."

"I assure you that it was all a mystery to him as it is to you and to all of us. Naturally he had no doubt that Wilson was guilty."

"You seem to know as much about it as if you were there, sir."

"I worked with Sir James in the arsenal at Woolwich."

"I see. You cannot throw any new light upon the affair then?"

"I know nothing myself save what I have read or heard. I have no desire to be discourteous, but you can understand, Mr. Holmes, that we are much disturbed at present, and I must ask you to hasten this interview to an end."

"This is indeed an unexpected development," said my friend when we had regained the cab. "I wonder if the death was natural, or whether the poor old fellow killed himself! If the latter, may it be taken as some sign of self-reproach for duty neglected? We must leave that question to the future.

"Come, Watson," said he, "our ways lie elsewhere. Our next station must be the office from which the papers were taken. It was black enough and our inquiries make it blacker," he remarked as the cab lumbered off. "It is all very bad."

"But surely, Holmes, character goes for something? Why should Wilson commit a treasonous felony and what has Sir James death got to do with it?"

"Exactly! There are certainly objections. But it is a formidable case which they have to meet."

Mr. Sidney Johnson, the senior clerk, met us at the office and received us with that respect which my companion's card always commanded. He was a thin, gruff, bespectacled man of middle age, his cheeks haggard, and his hands twitching from the nervous strain to which he had been subjected.

"It is bad, Mr. Holmes, very bad! Have you heard of the death of the chief?"

"We have just come from his house."

"The place is disorganised. The chief dead and the treaty stolen. And yet, when we closed our door on Monday evening, we were as efficient an office as any in the government service. Good God, it is dreadful to think of! That Wilson, of all men, should have done such a thing!"

"You are sure of his guilt, then?"

"I can see no other way out of it. And yet I would have trusted him as I trust myself."

"At what hour was the office closed on Monday?"

"At five."

"Did you close it?"

"I am always the last man out."

"Where were the papers?"

"In that safe. I had put them there myself weeks ago."

"Is there no watchman to the building?"

"There is, but he has other departments to look after as well. He is an old soldier and a most trustworthy man. He saw nothing that evening. Of course the fog was very thick."

"Suppose that Wilson wished to make his way into the building after hours; he would need three keys, would he not, before he could reach the papers?"

"Yes, he would. The key of the outer door, the key of the office, and the key of the safe."

"Only Sir James Walter and you had those keys?"

"I had no keys of the doors--only of the safe."

"Was Sir James a man who was orderly in his habits?"

"Yes, I think he was. I know that so far as those three keys are concerned he kept them on the same ring. I have often seen them there."

"And that ring went with him to London?"

"He said so."

"And your key never left your possession?"

"Never."

"Then Wilson, if he is the culprit, must have had a duplicate. And yet none was found upon his body."

"Singular, no doubt--and yet it seems he did so."

"Every inquiry in this case reveals something inexplicable. Now, there are some articles from the treaty still missing. They are, as I understand, the vital ones."

"I have no idea what you mean."

"No? Very good."

"I think, with your permission, I will now take a stroll round the premises. I do not recall any other question which I desired to ask."

He examined the lock of the safe, the door of the room, and finally the iron shutters of the window. It was only when we were on the lawn outside that his interest was strongly excited. There was a laurel bush outside the window, and several of the branches bore signs of having been twisted or snapped. He examined them carefully with his lens, and then some dim and vague marks upon the earth beneath. Finally he asked the chief clerk to close the iron shutters, and he pointed out to me that they hardly met in the centre, and that it would be possible for anyone outside to see what was going on within the room.

"The indications are ruined by three days' delay. They may mean something or nothing. Well, Watson, I do not think that Woolwich can help us further. It is a small crop which we have gathered. Let us see if we can do better in London."

Yet we added one more sheaf to our harvest before we left Woolwich Station. The clerk in the ticket office was able to say with confidence that he saw the military figure of Wilson--whom he clearly identified by both his uniform and the photo we showed him--upon the Monday night, and that he purchased a ticket for the 6:15 to London Bridge. He was alone and took a single third-class ticket. The clerk was struck at the time by his excited and nervous manner. So shaky was he that he could hardly pick up his change, and the clerk had helped him with it. A reference to the timetable showed that the 6:15 was the first train which it was possible for Wilson to take after the office had been closed at 5:00.

"Let us reconstruct, Watson," said Holmes after half an hour of silence. "I am not aware that in all our joint researches we have ever had a case which was more difficult to get at. Every fresh advance which we make only reveals a fresh ridge beyond. And yet we have surely made some appreciable progress.

"The effect of our inquiries at Woolwich has in the main been negligible and still against Wilson; but the indications at the window would lend themselves to a more favourable hypothesis. Let us suppose, for example, that he had been approached by some foreign agent or that he happened to notice someone looking suspicious near the offices. Any one of a thousand reasons we may never know could account for why he had been in the area. Very good. We will now suppose he suddenly, in the fog, caught a glimpse of this agent going in the direction of the office. He was an impetuous man, quick in his decisions. Everything gave way to his duty. He followed the man, reached the window, saw the abstraction of the documents, and pursued the thief. So far it holds together."

"What is the next step?"

"Then we come into difficulties. One would imagine that under such circumstances the first act of Wilson would be to seize the villain and raise the alarm. Why did he not do so? Could it have been a senior official who took the papers? That would explain Wilson's conduct and maybe Sir James' death. Or could the thief have given Wilson the slip in the fog, and Wilson started at once to London to head him off from his own rooms, presuming that he knew where the rooms were? Our scent runs cold here, and there is a vast gap between either hypothesis and the murder of Wilson found with some of the treaty papers in his pocket, on the steps to his house. My instinct now is to work from the other end."

"You are off?"

"Yes, I will while away the time at Godolphin Street with our friends of the regular establishment. With James Larrabee may lie the solution of our problem, though I must admit that I have not an inkling as to what form it may take. It is a capital mistake to theorize in advance of the facts. Do you stay on guard at our rooms, my good Watson, and receive any fresh visitors? I will join you when I am able."

All that day and the next and the next Holmes was in a mood which his friends would call taciturn, and others morose. He ran out and ran in, smoked incessantly, played snatches on his violin, sank into reveries, devoured sandwiches at irregular hours, and hardly answered the casual questions which I put to him. It was evident to me that things were not going well with him or his quest. He would say nothing of the case, and it was from the papers that I learned the particulars of the inquest, and the arrest with the subsequent release of John Mitton, the valet of the deceased. The coroner's jury brought in the obvious Wilful Murder, but the parties remained as unknown as ever. No motive was suggested. The room was full of articles of value, but none had been taken. The dead man's papers had not been tampered with. They were carefully examined, and showed that he was a keen student of international politics, an indefatigable gossip, a remarkable linguist, and an untiring letter writer. He had been on intimate terms with the leading politicians of several countries. But nothing sensational was discovered among the documents which filled his drawers. As to his relations with women, they appeared to have been promiscuous but superficial. He had many acquaintances among them, but few friends, and no one whom he loved. His habits were regular, his conduct inoffensive. His death was an absolute mystery and likely to remain so.

As to the arrest of John Mitton, the valet, it was a council of despair as an alternative to absolute inaction. But no case could be sustained against him. He had visited friends in Hammersmith that night. The alibi was complete. It is true that he started home at an hour which should have brought him to Westminster before the time when the crime was discovered, but his own explanation that he had walked part of the way seemed probable enough. He had actually arrived at twelve o'clock, and appeared to be overwhelmed by the unexpected tragedy. He had always been on good terms with his master. Several of the dead man's possessions—notably a small case of razors—had been found in the valet's boxes, but he explained that they had been presents from the deceased, and the housekeeper was able to corroborate the story. Mitton had been in Larrabee's employment for three years. It was noticeable that Larrabee did not take Mitton on the Continent with him. Sometimes he visited Paris for three months on end, but Mitton was left in charge of the Godolphin Street house. As to the housekeeper, she had heard nothing on the night of the crime. If her master had a visitor he had himself admitted him.

So for three mornings the mysteries remained, so far as I could follow them in the papers. If Holmes knew more, he kept his own counsel, but, as he told me that Inspector Lestrade had taken him into his confidence in the Larrabee case, I knew that he was in close touch with every development. Upon the fourth day there appeared a long telegram from Paris which seemed to solve the whole question.

I read the following account in the Daily Telegraph.

A discovery has just been made by the Parisian police which raises the veil which hung round the tragic fate of Mr. James Larrabee, who met his death by violence last Monday night at Godolphin Street, Westminster. Our readers will remember that the deceased gentleman was found stabbed in his room, and that some suspicion attached to his valet, but that the case broke down on an alibi. Yesterday a lady, who has been known as Mme. Henri Fournaye, occupying a small villa in the Rue Austerlitz, was reported to the authorities by her servants as being insane. An examination showed she had indeed developed mania of a dangerous and permanent form. On inquiry, the police have discovered that Mme. Henri Fournaye only returned from a journey to London on Tuesday last, and there is evidence to connect her with the crime at Westminster. A comparison of photographs has proved conclusively that M. Henri Fournaye and James Larrabee were really one and the same person, and that

51

the deceased had for some reason lived a double life in London and Paris. Mme. Fournaye, who is of Creole origin, is of an extremely excitable nature, and has suffered in the past from attacks of jealousy which have amounted to frenzy. It is conjectured that it was in one of these that she committed the terrible crime which has caused such a sensation in London. Her movements upon the Monday night have not yet been traced, but it is undoubted that a woman answering to her description attracted much attention at Charing Cross Station on Tuesday morning by the wildness of her appearance and the violence of her gestures. It is probable, therefore, that the crime was either committed when insane, or that its immediate effect was to drive the unhappy woman out of her mind. At present she is unable to give any coherent account of the past, and the doctors hold out no hopes of the reestablishment of her reason. There is evidence that a woman, who might have been Mme. Fournaye, was seen for some hours upon Monday night watching the house in Godolphin Street.

"What do you think of that, Holmes?" I had read the account aloud to him, while he finished his breakfast.

"My dear Watson," said he, as he rose from the table and paced up and down the room, "You are most long-suffering, but if I have told you nothing in the last three days, it is because there is nothing to tell. Even now this report from Paris does not help us much."

"Surely it is final as regards the man's death."

"The man's death is a mere incident—a trivial episode—in comparison with our real task, which is to trace the secret articles of the treaty and avert a European catastrophe. Only one important thing has happened in the last three days, and that is that nothing has happened. I get reports almost hourly from the government, and it is certain that nowhere in Europe is there any sign of the treaty. Now, if this treaty were loose—no, it CAN NOT be loose—but if it is not loose, where can it be? Who has it? Why is it held back? That is the question that beats in my brain like a hammer. Was it, indeed, a coincidence that Larrabee should meet his death on the night when the treaty disappeared? Did the treaty ever reach him? If so, why is it not among his papers? Did this mad wife of his carry it off with her? If so, is it in her house in Paris? How could I search for it without the French police having their suspicions aroused? It is a case, my dear Watson, where the law is as dangerous to us as the criminals are. Every man's hand is against us, and yet the interests at stake are colossal. Should I bring it to a successful conclusion, it will certainly represent the crowning glory of my career. Ah, here is my latest from the front!" He glanced hurriedly at the note which had been handed in. "Halloa! Lestrade seems to have observed something of interest. Put on your hat, Watson, and we will stroll down together to Westminster."

It was my first visit to the scene of the Larrabee murder—a high, dingy, narrow-chested house, prim, formal, and solid, like the century which gave it birth. Lestrade's bulldog features gazed out at us from the front window, and he greeted us warmly when a big constable had opened the door and let us in. The room into which we were shown was that in which the crime had been committed, but no trace of it now remained save an ugly, irregular stain upon the carpet. This carpet was a small square drugget in the centre of the room, surrounded by a broad expanse of beautiful, old-fashioned wood-flooring in square blocks, highly polished. Over the fireplace was a magnificent trophy of weapons, one of which had been used on that tragic night. In the window was a sumptuous writing-desk, and every detail of the apartment, the pictures, the rugs, and the hangings, all pointed to a taste which was luxurious to the verge of effeminacy.

"Seen the Paris news?" asked Lestrade.

Holmes nodded.

"Our French friends seem to have touched the spot this time. No doubt it's just as they say. She knocked at the door—surprise visit, I guess, for he kept his life in water-tight compartments—he let her in, couldn't keep her in the street. She told him how she had traced him, reproached him. One thing led to another, and then with that dagger so handy the end soon came. It wasn't all done in an instant, though, for these chairs were all swept over yonder, and he had one in his hand as if he had tried to hold her off with it. We've got it all clear as if we had seen it."

Holmes raised his eyebrows.

"And yet you have sent for me?"

"Ah, yes, that's another matter—a mere trifle, but the sort of thing you take an interest in—queer, you know, and what you might call freakish. It has nothing to do with the main fact—can't have, on the face of it."

"What is it, then?"

"Well, you know, after a crime of this sort we are very careful to keep things in their position. Nothing has been moved. Officer in charge here day and night. This morning, as the man was buried and the investigation over—so far as this room is concerned—we thought we could tidy up a bit. This carpet. You see, it is not fastened down, only just laid there. We had occasion to raise it. We found—"

"Yes? You found—"

Holmes's face grew tense with anxiety.

"Well, I'm sure you would never guess in a hundred years what we did find. You see that stain on the carpet? Well, a great deal must have soaked through, must it not?"

"Undoubtedly it must."

"Well, you will be surprised to hear that there is no stain on the white woodwork to correspond."

"No stain! But there must—"

"Yes, so you would say. But the fact remains that there isn't."

He took the corner of the carpet in his hand and, turning it over, he showed that it was indeed as he said.

"But the under side is as stained as the upper. It must have left a mark."

Lestrade chuckled with delight at having puzzled the famous expert.

"Now, I'll show you the explanation. There IS a second stain, but it does not correspond with the other. See for yourself." As he spoke he turned over another portion of the carpet, and there, sure enough, was a great crimson spill upon the square white facing of the old-fashioned floor. "What do you make of that, Mr. Holmes?"

"Why, it is simple enough. The two stains did correspond, but the carpet has been turned round. As it was square and unfastened it was easily done."

"The official police don't need you, Mr. Holmes, to tell them that the carpet must have been turned round. That's clear enough, for the stains lie above each other—if you lay it over this way. But what I want to know is, who shifted the carpet, and why?"

I could see from Holmes's rigid face that he was vibrating with inward excitement.

"Look here, Lestrade," said he, "has that constable in the passage been in charge of the place all the time?"

"Yes, he has."

"Well, take my advice. Examine him carefully. Do not do it before us. We will wait here. You take him into the back room. You will be more likely to get a confession out of him alone. Ask him how he dared to admit people and leave them alone in this room. Do not ask him if he has done it. Take it for granted. Tell him you KNOW someone has been here. Press him. Tell him that a full confession is his only chance of forgiveness. Do exactly what I tell you!"

"By George, if he knows I'll have it out of him!" cried Lestrade. He darted into the hall, and a few moments later his bullying voice sounded from the back room.

"Now, Watson, now!" cried Holmes with frenzied eagerness. All the demoniacal force of the man masked behind that listless manner burst out in a paroxysm of energy. He tore the drugget from the floor, and in an instant was down on his hands and knees clawing at each of the squares of wood beneath it. One turned sideways as he dug his nails into the edge of it. It hinged back like the lid of a box. A small black cavity opened beneath it. Holmes plunged his eager hand into it and drew it out with a bitter snarl of anger and disappointment. It was empty.

"Quick, Watson, quick! Get it back again!" The wooden lid was replaced, and the drugget had only just been drawn straight when Lestrade's voice was heard in the passage. He found Holmes leaning languidly against the mantelpiece, resigned and patient, endeavouring to conceal his irrepressible yawns.

"Sorry to keep you waiting, Mr. Holmes, I can see that you are bored to death with the whole affair. Well, he has confessed, all right. Come in here, MacPherson. Let these gentlemen hear of your most inexcusable conduct."

The big constable, hot and penitent, sidled into the room.

"I meant no harm, sir, I'm sure. The young woman came to the door last evening—mistook the house, she did. And then we got talking. It's lonesome, when you're on duty here all day."

"Well, what happened then?"

"She wanted to see where the crime was done—had read about it in the papers, she said. She was a respectable, well-spoken young woman, sir, and I saw no harm in letting her have a peep. When she saw that mark on the carpet, down she dropped on the floor, and lay as if she were dead. I ran to the back and got some water, but I could not bring her to. Then I went round the corner to the Ivy Plant for some brandy, and by the time I had brought it back the young woman had recovered and was off—ashamed of herself, I daresay, and dared not face me."

"How about moving that drugget?"

"Well, sir, it was a bit rumpled, certainly, when I came back. You see, she fell on it and it lies on a polished floor with nothing to keep it in place. I straightened it out afterwards."

"It's a lesson to you that you can't deceive me, Constable MacPherson," said Lestrade, with dignity. "No doubt you thought that your breach of duty could never be discovered, and yet a mere glance at that drugget was enough to convince me that someone had been admitted to the room. It's lucky for you, my man, that nothing is missing, or you would find yourself in Queer Street. I'm sorry to have called you down over such a petty business, Mr. Holmes, but I thought the point of the second stain not corresponding with the first would interest you."

"Certainly, it was most interesting. Has this woman only been here once, constable?"

"Yes, sir, only once."

"Who was she?"

"Don't know the name, sir. Was answering an advertisement about typewriting and came to the wrong number—very pleasant, genteel young woman, sir."

"Tall? Handsome?"

"Yes, sir, she was a well-grown young woman. I suppose you might say she was handsome. Perhaps some would say she was very handsome. 'Oh, officer, do let me have a peep!' says she. She had pretty, coaxing ways, as you might say, and I thought there was no harm in letting her just put her head through the door."

"How was she dressed?"

"Quiet, sir—a long mantle down to her feet."

"What time was it?"

"It was just growing dusk at the time. They were lighting the lamps as I came back with the brandy."

"Very good," said Holmes. "Come, Watson, I think that we have more important work elsewhere."

As we left the house Lestrade remained in the front room, while the repentant constable opened the door to let us out. Holmes turned on the step and held up something in his hand. The constable stared intently.

"Good Lord, sir!" he cried, with amazement on his face. Holmes put his finger on his lips, replaced his hand in his breast pocket, and burst out laughing as we turned down the street. "Excellent!" said he. "Come, friend Watson, the curtain rings up for the next act. You will be relieved to hear that this incident is explained and is unrelated to the loss of the treaty or the murder of Wilson. Unfortunately, we must still act to ensure there will be no war, that Sir Edward and the Chancellor will suffer no setbacks in their brilliant careers, that Sir James' and the Field-Marshal's names may be cleared if they are innocent, that Prime Minister Asquith will have no European complication to deal with, and that with a little tact and management upon our part nobody will be a penny the worse for what might have been a very ugly incident."

My mind filled with admiration for this extraordinary man.

"You have solved it!" I cried.

"Hardly that, Watson. There are many points which are as dark as ever. But we have enough that it will be our own fault if we cannot get the rest. There remain only two men on our list and with their addresses we may be able to pick our man and follow two tracks instead of one."

Chapter 4: To catch a thief

"Well, well," said Holmes presently with an exclamation of satisfaction, "things are turning a little in our direction at last." He had spread out his big map of London and leaned eagerly over it. "While there are numerous small fry, there are but few who would handle so big an affair. The only men left worth considering are; Louis La Rothiere, of Campden Mansions, Notting Hill; and Hugo Oberstein, 13 Caulfield Gardens, Kensington. Why, Watson, I do honestly believe that we are going to pull it off, after all."

He slapped me on the shoulder with a sudden burst of hilarity. "I am going out now. It is only a reconnaissance. I will do nothing serious without my trusted comrade and biographer at my elbow. Do stay here, and the odds are that you will see me again in an hour or two. If time hangs heavy get foolscap and a pen, and begin your narrative of how we saved the State."

I felt some reflection of his elation in my own mind, for I knew well that he would not depart so far from his usual austerity of demeanour unless there was good cause for exultation. All the long evening I waited, filled with impatience for his return. At last, shortly after nine o'clock, there arrived a messenger with a note:

Am dining at Goldini's
Restaurant, Gloucester
Road, Kensington.
Please come at once and
join me there. Bring with

you a jemmy, a dark
lantern, a chisel, and a
revolver.

S. H.

It was a nice equipment for a respectable citizen to carry through the dim, fog-draped streets. I stowed them all discreetly away in my overcoat and drove straight to the address given. There sat my friend at a little round table near the door of the garish Italian restaurant.

"Have you had something to eat? Then join me in a coffee and curacao. Try one of the proprietor's cigars. They are less poisonous than one would expect. Have you the tools?"

"They are here, in my overcoat."

"Excellent. Let me give you a short sketch of what I have done, with some indication of what we are about to do. Now it must be evident to you, Watson, that Larrabee's death is in no way related to Wilson or to the missing part of the treaty. It is concerned with some love affair, a romantic entanglement or some scandal, and with blackmail no doubt. We may look into it after we have handled these more pressing matters. That was clear from the instant that I determined the fact that it was Irene Adler who so cleverly made her way into Larrabee's apartment after his death. I was not surprised that she was in some way involved in it!"

"Was it her picture you showed to Constable MacPherson?"

"Indeed it was my dear Watson."

"It seems most improbable."

"Yes, Watson, we must fall back upon the old axiom that when all other contingencies fail, whatever remains, however improbable, must be the truth. Here all other contingencies HAVE failed. Once that was cleared up and Larrabbe's name untangled from this skein, it left only two names on our list: La Rothiere, in Notting Hill and Oberstein in Kensington. Which one of the two is it? That was the question which we had to answer. There was only one possible way. I had to go round and see who was in residence and who was not. When I found La Rothiere was at home and that the other leading international agent had recently left London, Mr. Hugo Oberstein, of 13 Caulfield Gardens, had become my objective."

"Splendid, Holmes! You have got it!"

"So far--so far, Watson. We advance, but the goal is afar. Oberstein lived there with a single valet, who was probably a confederate entirely in his confidence. We must bear in mind that Oberstein has gone to the Continent to dispose of his booty, but not with any idea of flight; for he had no reason to fear a warrant, and the idea of an amateur domiciliary visit would certainly never occur to him. Yet that is precisely what we are about to make."

"Could we not get a warrant and legalize it?"

"Hardly on the evidence."

"What can we hope to do?"

"We cannot tell what correspondence may be there."

"I don't like it, Holmes."

"My dear fellow, you shall keep watch in the street. I will do the criminal part. It is not a time to stick at trifles. Think of Mycroft's note, of the Admiralty, the Cabinet, the exalted persons who wait for news. We are bound to go."

My answer was to rise from the table.

"You are right, Holmes. We are bound to go."

He sprang up and shook me by the hand.

"I knew you would not shrink at the last," said he, and for a moment I saw something in his eyes which was nearer to tenderness than I had ever seen. The next instant he was his masterful, practical self once more.

"It is nearly half a mile, but there is no hurry. Let us walk," said he. "Do not drop the instruments, I beg. Your arrest as a suspicious character would be a most unfortunate complication."

Caulfield Gardens was one of those lines of flat-faced pillared, and porticoed houses which are so prominent a product of the middle Victorian epoch in the West End of London. Next door there appeared to be a children's party, for the merry buzz of young voices and the clatter of a piano resounded through the night. The fog still hung about and screened us with its friendly shade. Holmes had lit his lantern and flashed it upon the massive door.

"This is a serious proposition," said he. "It is certainly bolted as well as locked. We would do better in the area. There is an excellent archway down yonder in case a too zealous policeman should intrude. Give me a hand, Watson, and I will do the same for you."

A minute later we were both in the area. Hardly had we reached the dark shadows before the step of the policeman was heard in the fog above. As its soft rhythm died away, Holmes set to work upon the lower door. I saw him stoop and strain until with a sharp crash it flew open. We sprang through into the dark passage, closing the area door behind us.

"Here we are, Watson--this must be the one."

Holmes swept his light along the door-frame.

"You can see where they rested the body. Halloa, Watson! what is this? There can be no doubt that it is a blood mark."

He was pointing to faint discolourations along the woodwork of the floor.

"Here it is on the stone of the stair also. The demonstration is complete. So far we are justified," said he. "What do you think of it, Watson?"

"A masterpiece. You have never risen to a greater height."

"I cannot agree with you there. .... If it were not for the grave interests involved, the affair up to this point would be insignificant. Our difficulties are still before us. But perhaps we may find something here which may help us."

We had ascended the kitchen stair and entered the suite of rooms upon the first floor. One was a dining-room, severely furnished and containing nothing of interest. A second was a bedroom, which also drew blank. The remaining room appeared more promising, and my companion settled down to a systematic examination. It was littered with books and papers, and was evidently used as a study. Swiftly and methodically Holmes turned over the contents of drawer after drawer and cupboard after cupboard, but no gleam of success came to brighten his austere face. At the end of an hour he was no further than when he started.

"The cunning dog has covered his tracks," said he. "He has left nothing to incriminate him. His dangerous correspondence has been destroyed or removed. This is our last chance."

It was a small tin cash-box which stood upon the writing-desk. Holmes pried it open with his chisel. Several rolls of paper were within, covered with figures and calculations, without any note to show to what they referred. Holmes tossed them all impatiently aside. There only remained an envelope with some small newspaper slips inside it. He shook them out on the table, and at once I saw by his eager face that his hopes had been raised.

"What is this, Watson? Eh? What is this? Record of a series of messages in the advertisements of a paper. Daily

Telegraph agony column by the print and paper. Right-hand top corner of a page. No dates--but messages arrange themselves. This must be the first:

> "Hoped to hear sooner. Terms
> agreed to. Write fully to address
> given on card.
> "Pierrot.
> "Next comes:
> "Too complex for description.
> Must have full report, Stuff awaits
> you when goods delivered.
> "Pierrot.
> "Then comes:
> "Matter presses. Must withdraw
> offer unless contract completed.
> Make appointment by letter. Will
> confirm by advertisement.
> "Pierrot.
> "Finally:
> "Monday night after nine. Two
> taps. Only ourselves. Do not be so
> suspicious. "Payment in hard cash
> when goods delivered.
> "Pierrot.

"A fairly complete record, Watson! If we could only get at the man at the other end!" He sat lost in thought, tapping his fingers on the table. Finally he sprang to his feet.

"Well, perhaps it will not be so difficult, after all. There is nothing more to be done here, Watson. I think we might drive round to the offices of the Daily Telegraph, and so bring a good day's work to a conclusion."

Mycroft Holmes had come round by appointment after breakfast next day and Sherlock Holmes had recounted to him our proceedings of the day before. His brother shook his head over our confessed burglary.

"We cannot do these things in the name of Government, Sherlock," said he. "No wonder you get results that are beyond us."

"For England, home and beauty--eh, Watson? Martyrs on the altar of our country. But what do you think of it, Mycroft?"

"Excellent, Sherlock! Admirable! But what use will you make of it?"

Holmes picked up the Daily Telegraph which lay upon the table.

"Have you seen Pierrot's advertisement to-day?"

"What? Another one?"

"Yes, here it is."

> To-night. Same hour.
> Same place. Two taps.
> Most vitally important.
> Your own safety at
> stake.
> Pierrot.

"By George!" I cried. "If he answers that we've got him!"

"That was my idea when I put it in. I think if you could both make it convenient to come with me about eight o'clock to Caulfield Gardens we might possibly get a little nearer to a solution."

I remember that during the whole of that memorable day he lost himself in a monograph which he had undertaken upon Palestrina Style Counterpoint. For my own part I had none of this power of detachment, and the day, in consequence, appeared to be interminable. The great national importance of the issue, the suspense in high quarters, the direct nature of the experiment which we were trying--all combined to work upon my nerve. It was a relief to me when at last, after a light dinner, we set out upon our expedition. Mycroft met us by appointment at the outside of Gloucester Road Station. The area door of Oberstein's house had been left open the night before, and it was necessary for me, as Mycroft Holmes absolutely and indignantly declined to climb the railings, to pass in and open the hall door. By nine o'clock we were all seated in the study, waiting patiently for our man.

An hour passed and yet another. When eleven struck, the measured beat of the great church clock seemed to sound the dirge of our hopes. Mycroft and I were fidgeting in our seats and looking twice a minute at our watches. Holmes sat silent and composed, his eyelids half shut, but every sense on the alert. He raised his head with a sudden jerk.

"He is coming," said he.

There had been a furtive step past the door. Now it returned. We heard a shuffling sound outside, and then two sharp taps with the knocker. Holmes rose, motioning us to remain seated. The gas in the hall was a mere point of light. He opened the outer door, and then as a dark figure slipped past him he closed and fastened it. "This way!" we heard him say, and a moment later our man stood before us. Holmes had followed him closely, and as the man turned with a cry of surprise and alarm he caught him by the collar and threw him back into the room. Before our prisoner had recovered his balance the door was shut and Holmes standing with his back against it. The man glared round him, staggered, and fell senseless upon the floor. With the shock, his broad-brimmed hat flew from his head, his cravat slipped down from his lips, and there were the long light beard and the soft, handsome delicate features of Colonel Valentine Walter.

Holmes gave a whistle of surprise.

"You can write me down an ass this time, Watson," said he. "This was not the bird that I was looking for."

"Who is he?" asked Mycroft eagerly.

"The younger brother of the late Sir James Walter. Yes, yes; I see the fall of the cards. He is coming to. I think that you had best leave his examination to me."

We had carried the prostrate body to the sofa. Now our prisoner sat up, looked round him with a horror-stricken face, and passed his hand over his forehead, like one who cannot believe his own senses.

"What is this?" he asked. "I came here to visit Mr. Oberstein."

"Everything is known, Colonel Walter," said Holmes. "How an English gentleman could behave in such a manner is beyond my comprehension. But your whole correspondence and relations with Oberstein are within our knowledge. So also are the circumstances connected with the death of Field-Marshal Wilson. Let me advise you to gain at least the small credit for repentance and confession, since there are still some details which we can only learn from your lips."

The man groaned and sank his face in his hands. We waited, but he was silent.

"I can assure you," said Holmes, "that every essential is already known. We know that you were pressed for money; that you took an impress of the keys which your brother held; and that you entered into a correspondence with Oberstein, who answered your letters through the advertisement columns of the Daily Telegraph. We are aware that you went down to the office in the fog on Monday night, but that you were seen and followed by Wilson. He saw your theft, but could not give the alarm, as it was just possible that you were taking the treaty to your brother in London and he was aware of the parts of the treaty that had to remain secret. Leaving all his private concerns, like the good soldier that he was, he followed you closely in the fog and kept at your heels until you reached this very house. There he intervened, and then it was, Colonel Walter, that to treason you added the terrible crime of murder."

"I did not! I did not! Before God I swear that I did not!" cried our wretched prisoner.

"Tell us, then, how Field-Marshal Henry Wilson met his end before you laid him upon the steps to his home."

"I will. I swear to you that I will. I did the rest. I confess it. It was just as you say. A Stock Exchange debt had to be paid. I needed the money badly. Oberstein offered me five thousand. It was to save myself from ruin. But as to murder, I am as innocent as you."

"What happened, then?"

"Wilson followed me as you describe. I never knew it until I was at the very door. It was thick fog, and one could not see three yards. I had given two taps and Oberstein had come to the door. Wilson rushed up and demanded the return of the papers. Oberstein had a short life-preserver. He always carried it with him. As Wilson forced his way after us into the house Oberstein struck him on the head. The blow was a fatal one. He was dead within five minutes. There he lay in the hall, and we were at our wit's end what to do. First Oberstein examined the treaty papers which I had brought. He said that some of them were essential, and that he must keep them. 'You cannot keep them,' said I. 'There will be a dreadful row at Woolwich if they are not returned.' 'I must keep them,' said he, 'for a copy will be no proof of their existence.' 'Then they must all go back together to-night,' said I. He thought for a little, and then he cried out that he had it. 'These I will keep,' said he. 'The others we will stuff into the pocket of this man. When he is

found the whole business will assuredly be put to his account.'
I could see no other way out of it, so we did as he suggested.
We waited half an hour at the window before all traffic
stopped. It was so thick that nothing could be seen, and we had
no difficulty in transporting Wilson's body on a cart the two
miles to his home in Knightsbridge. That was the end of the
matter so far as I was concerned."

"And your brother?"

"He said nothing, but he had caught me once with his
keys, and I think that he suspected. I read in his eyes that he
suspected. As you know, he never held up his head again."

There was silence in the room. It was broken by
Mycroft Holmes.

"Can you not make reparation? It would ease your
conscience, and possibly your punishment."

"What reparation can I make?"

"Where is Oberstein with the papers?"

"I do not know."

"Did he give you no address?"

"He said that letters to the Hotel du Louvre, Paris,
would eventually reach him."

"Then reparation is still within your power," said
Sherlock Holmes.

"I will do anything I can. I owe this fellow no
particular good-will. He has been my ruin and my downfall."

"Here are paper and pen. Sit at this desk and write to
my dictation. Direct the envelope to the address given. That is
right. Now the letter:

"Dear Sir:

"With regard to our transaction,
you will no doubt have observed

by now that one essential detail is missing. I have information which will make it complete. This has involved me in extra trouble, however, and I must ask you for a further advance of five hundred pounds. I will not trust it to the post, nor will I take anything but gold or notes. I would come to you abroad, but it would excite remark if I left the country at present. Therefore I shall expect to meet you in the smoking-room of the Charing Cross Hotel at noon on Saturday. Remember that only English notes, or gold, will be taken."

"That will do very well. I shall be very much surprised if it does not fetch our man."

And it did! It is a matter of history--that secret history of a nation which is often so much more intimate and interesting than its public chronicles--that Oberstein, eager to complete the coup of his lifetime, came to the lure and was safely engulfed for fifteen years in a British prison. We never found the secret articles from the treaty and can only assume

71

the worst. Colonel Walter died in prison towards the end of the second year of his sentence. As to Holmes, he returned refreshed to his monograph upon Palestrina Style Counterpoint, which has since been printed for private circulation, and is said by experts to be the last word upon the subject. He said no more about the treaty; but I fancy that I could guess what he thought a month later. In the meantime, we had two loose ends that remained to be tied up: one was the threatened gold reserves, the other, the mystery of Irene Adler and James Larrabee.

Chapter 5: The Gold Robbery

"Sarasate plays at the St. James's Hall this afternoon," Holmes remarked the next morning. "What do you think, Watson? Could your patients spare you for a few more hours?"

"I have nothing to do to-day. My practice is never very absorbing."

"Then put on your hat and come. I am going through the City first, and we can have some lunch on the way. I observe that there is a good deal of German music on the programme, which is rather more to my taste than Italian or French. It is introspective, and I want to introspect. Come along!"

We travelled by the Underground as far as Westminster; and a short walk took us down Whitehall and Downing Streets, then on to St James Park, singularly lovely; a splendid park with fine old timber surrounding two buildings at its edge, and the lake lay close to the avenue. The far-ground was covered with golden patches of flowering gorse, gleaming magnificently in the light of the bright summer sunshine.

It was the park offices that occupied Holmes' attention where two brick houses looked out into the lake and on to a railed-in enclosure, and where extensive gardens surrounded three sides of the cottages. The immediate area surrounding the houses, however, was so thick with dirt in irregular mounds and curious earthworks which hinted at some strife. The whole place, with its scattered dirt-heaps and ill-grown shrubs, had a blighted, ill-omened look and bore the foreshadowed reflection of some great disaster. Several garden and digging implements lay about. Sherlock Holmes stopped in front of it with his head on one side and looked it all over, with his eyes shining brightly between puckered lids. Then he walked slowly up the footpath and then the street, and then down again to the corner, still looking keenly at the little offices and the nearby houses of Parliament and back toward Downing Street. Finally he returned to the offices, and, having thumped vigorously upon the pavement with his stick two or three times, he went up to the door of the nearest and knocked. It was eventually opened by a bright-looking, clean-shaven young fellow, who asked him to step in.

"Thank you," said Holmes, "I only wished to ask you how you would go from here to Trafalgar Square."

"Third right, fourth left," answered the man promptly, closing the door.

"Smart fellow, that," observed Holmes as we walked away. "He is, in my judgment, the fourth smartest man in London, and for daring I am not sure that he has not a claim to be third. I have known something of him before."

"Evidently," said I, "you consider this place counts for a good deal in this mystery of the French Gold. I am sure that you inquired your way merely in order that you might see this man."

"Not him. I already knew what he looks like. He is small, stout-built, very quick in his ways, no hair on his face, though he's not short of thirty. Has a white splash of acid upon his forehead and his ears are pierced for earrings."

"What then?"

"The knees of his trousers."

"And what did you see?"

"What I expected to see."

"Why did you beat the pavement?"

"My dear doctor, this is a time for observation, not for talk. We are spies in an enemy's country. We know something of the lay of the land. And now, Doctor, we have done our work, so it is time we had some play. A sandwich and a cup of coffee, and then off to violin-land, where all is sweetness and delicacy and harmony, and there are no clients to vex us with their conundrums."

My friend was an enthusiastic musician, being himself not only a capable performer but a composer of no ordinary merit. All the afternoon he sat in the stalls wrapped in the most perfect happiness, gently waving his long, thin fingers in time to the music, while his gently smiling face and his languid, dreamy eyes were as unlike those of Holmes the sleuth-hound, Holmes the relentless, keen-witted, ready-handed criminal agent, as it was possible to conceive. In his singular character the dual nature alternately asserted itself, and his extreme exactness and astuteness represented, as I have often thought, the reaction against the poetic and contemplative mood which occasionally predominated in him. The swing of his nature took him from extreme languor to devouring energy; and, as I knew well, he was never so truly formidable as when, for days on end, he had been lounging in his armchair amid his improvisations and his black-letter editions. Then it was that the lust of the chase would suddenly come upon him, and that his brilliant reasoning power would rise to the level of intuition, until those who were unacquainted with his methods would look askance at him as on a man whose knowledge was not that of other mortals. When I saw him that afternoon so enwrapped in the music at St. James's Hall I felt that an evil time might be coming upon those whom he had set himself to hunt down.

"You want to go home, no doubt, Doctor," he remarked as we emerged.

"Yes, it would be as well."

"This business at Downing Street is serious. A considerable crime is in contemplation. I have every reason to believe that we shall be in time to stop it."

We were very late in returning home—so late, that dinner was on the table when we appeared. At the end of our meal Holmes said, "The thing takes shape, Watson. It becomes coherent. Might I ask you to hand me my violin, and we will postpone all further thought upon this business until we have had the advantage of more music and contemplation. Let us try to forget for an hour this miserable waiting and the still more miserable ways of our fellow men."

A few moments later the long-drawn, wailing notes of that most haunting of tunes filled our rooms. For an hour he droned away upon his violin, endeavouring to soothe his own ruffled spirits as I tried to read one of Clark Russell's fine sea-stories.

"Do you remember what Darwin says about music?" he said, as he took his seat. "He claims that the power of producing and appreciating it existed among the human race long before the power of speech was arrived at. Perhaps that is why we are so subtly influenced by it. There are vague memories in our souls of those misty centuries when the world was in its childhood."

"That is rather a broad idea," I remarked.

"One's ideas must be as broad as Nature if they are to interpret Nature," he answered.

Later that evening Holmes sat motionless by the unlit fire, his hands buried deep in his trouser pockets, his chin sunk upon his breast, his eyes fixed upon the glowing embers in his pipe. For half an hour he was silent and still. Then, with the gesture of a man who has taken his decision, he sprang to his feet and passed into his bedroom. A little later a rakish young workman, with a goatee beard and a swagger, lit his clay pipe at the lamp before descending into the street. "I'll be back some time, Watson," said he, and vanished into the night. I understood that he had opened his campaign against the would-be gold thieves, but I little dreamed the strange shape which that campaign was destined to take.

For some days Holmes came and went at all hours in this attire, but beyond a remark that his time was spent at St. James Park, and that it was not wasted, I knew nothing of what he was doing. At last, however, on a wild, tempestuous evening, when the wind screamed and rattled against the windows, he returned from his last expedition, and having removed his disguise he sat before me and laughed heartily in his silent inward fashion.

"We must return to St. James Park one final time Watson," said Holmes.

We took a cab and when we arrived at the park we went up to the second of the two buildings we had seen a few days earlier and Holmes knocked at the door. The door opened, and the owner of the house, a rotund figure, presented himself.

"Mr. Josiah Brown, I suppose?" said Holmes.

"Yes, sir; and you, no doubt, are Mr. Sherlock Holmes? I had the note which you sent by the express messenger, and I did exactly what you told me. He is in the front office building as usual and he never returns until late. Well, I will be very glad to see that you have got the rascal. I hope, gentlemen, that you will come in and have some refreshment."

The portly man puffed out his chest with an appearance of some little pride. As he glanced at us, with his head thrust forward, I took a good look at the man and endeavoured, after the fashion of my companion, to read the indications which might be presented by his dress or appearance. I did not gain very much, however, by my inspection. The man bore every mark of being an average commonplace British tradesman, obese, pompous, and slow. He wore rather baggy grey shepherd's check trousers, a not over-clean black frock-coat, unbuttoned in the front, and a drab waistcoat with a heavy brassy Albert chain, and a square pierced bit of metal dangling down as an ornament. A frayed top-hat and a faded brown overcoat with a wrinkled velvet collar lay upon a hook behind him. Altogether, look as I would, there was nothing remarkable about the man save his blazing red head, and the expression of extreme chagrin and discontent upon his features.

Sherlock Holmes' quick eye took in my occupation, and he shook his head with a smile as he noticed my questioning glances. "Beyond the obvious facts that he has at some time done manual labour, that he takes snuff, that he is a Freemason, that he has been in China, and that he has done a considerable amount of writing lately, I can deduce nothing else."

Mr. Josiah Brown started up in his chair, with his eyes upon my companion.

"How, in the name of good-fortune, did you know all that, Mr. Holmes?" he asked. "How did you know, for example, that I did manual labour. It's as true as gospel, for I began as a gardener."

"Your hands, my dear sir. Your right hand is quite a size larger than your left. You have worked with it, and the muscles are more developed."

"Well, the snuff, then, and the Freemasonry?"

"I will not insult your intelligence by telling you how I read that, especially as, rather against the strict rules of your order, you use an arc-and-compass breastpin."

"Ah, of course, I forgot that. But the writing?"

"What else can be indicated by that right cuff so very shiny for five inches, and the left one with the smooth patch near the elbow where you rest it upon the desk?"

"Well, but China?"

"The fish that you have tattooed immediately above your right wrist could only have been done in China. I have made a small study of tattoo marks and have even contributed to the literature of the subject. That trick of staining the fishes' scales of a delicate pink is quite peculiar to China. When, in addition, I see a Chinese coin hanging from your watch-chain, the matter becomes even more simple."

Mr. Josiah Brown laughed heavily. "Well, I never!" said he. "I thought at first that you had done something clever, but I see that there was nothing in it after all."

"I begin to think, Watson," said Holmes, "that I make a mistake in explaining. '*Omne ignotum pro magnifico*,' you know, and my poor little reputation, such as it is, will suffer shipwreck if I am so candid. Can you answer one or two questions for us please Mr. Brown?"

"By all means," sad he.

"Please tell me about your establishment Mr. Brown."

"Well, Mr. Holmes," said Josiah Brown, mopping his forehead; "I am superintendent here at St. James Park. It's not a very large affair, and of late years it has not done more than just give me a living. I used to be able to keep two assistants, but now I only keep one; and I would have a job to pay him but that he is willing to come for half wages so as to learn the business."

"What is the name of this obliging youth?" asked Sherlock Holmes.

"His name is Prince Chetwood, and he's not such a youth, either. It's hard to say his age. I should not wish a smarter assistant, Mr. Holmes; and I know very well that he could better himself and earn twice what I am able to give him. But, after all, if he is satisfied, why should I put ideas in his head?"

"Why, indeed? You seem most fortunate in having an employee who comes under the full market price. It is not a common experience among employers in this age," remarked Holmes as his client paused and refreshed his memory with a huge pinch of snuff. "Pray continue your very interesting statement."

"Oh, he has his faults, too," said Mr. Wilson. "Never was such a fellow for photography. Snapping away with a camera when he ought to be improving his mind, and then diving down into the cellar like a rabbit into its hole to develop his pictures. That is his main fault, but on the whole he's a good worker. There's no vice in him."

"He lives with you, I presume?"

"Yes, sir. He and a girl of fourteen, who does a bit of simple cooking and keeps the place clean—that's all I have in the house, for I am a widower and never had any family. We three live in this back building and we use the front building as our offices. We live quietly, sir, the three of us; and we keep a roof over our heads and pay our debts, if we do nothing more."

"This assistant of yours—how long has he been with you?"

"About a month."

"How did he come?"

"In answer to an advertisement."

"Was he the only applicant?"

"No, I had a dozen."

"Why did you pick him?"

"Because he was handy and would come cheap."

"At half wages, in fact."

"Yes."

"Hum!" said Holmes, sinking back in deep thought. "He is in your front offices you say?"

"Oh, yes, sir; I have only just left him. As usual, he is working at his photography in the basement."

"All is as it should be then Mr. Brown," said Holmes. "I must ask you please, to remain here this evening, and we shall endeavour to clear up this episode as soon as possible."

"Well, Watson," said Holmes when we were settled in our cab on our way back to Baker Street, "what do you make of it all now?"

"I still make nothing of it," I answered frankly. "It is a most mysterious business."

"It grows less mysterious. But I must be prompt over this matter."

"What are you going to do, then?" I asked.

"I shall again want your help to-night."

"At what time?"

"Ten will be early enough. And, I say, Doctor, there may be some little danger, so kindly put your army revolver in your pocket before we leave."

I trust that I am not more dense than my neighbours, but I was always oppressed with a sense of my own stupidity in my dealings with Sherlock Holmes. Here I had heard what he had heard, I had seen what he had seen, and yet from his words it was evident that he saw clearly not only what had happened but what was about to happen, while to me the whole business was still confused and grotesque. As we made our way home to our rooms I thought over it all, from the extraordinary story of the French Gold to the warning cypher and the story of Mr. Josiah Brown. What was this nocturnal expedition, and why should I go armed? Where were we going, and what were we to do? I had the hint from Holmes that this smooth-faced assistant in the Park Offices was a formidable man—a man who might play a deep game. I tried to puzzle it out, but gave it up in despair and set the matter aside until night should bring an explanation.

It was a quarter-past nine when we returned to Baker Street. Holmes sent two telegraphs and sat smoking. At ten-o'clock we again descended our steps. A cab was standing at the door, and as we neared I heard the sound of voices from within. On entering, I found two men, one of whom I recognised as Peter Jones, the official police agent, while the other was a long, thin, sad-faced man, with a shiny hat and oppressively respectable frock-coat.

"Ha! Our party is complete," said Holmes, unbuttoning his pea-jacket and laying aside his heavy hunting crop he had brought with him from its rack. "Watson, I think you know Mr. Jones, of Scotland Yard? Let me introduce you to Sir John Simon, who is to be our companion in to-night's adventure."

"We're hunting in couples again, Doctor, you see," said Jones in his consequential way. "Our friend here is a wonderful man for starting a chase. All he wants is an old dog to help him to do the running down."

"I hope a wild goose may not prove to be the end of our chase," observed Sir John gloomily.

"You may place considerable confidence in Mr. Holmes, sir," said the police agent loftily. "He has his own little methods, which are, if he won't mind my saying so, just a little too theoretical and fantastic, but he has the makings of a detective in him. It is not too much to say that once or twice, as in that business of the Sholto murder and the Agra treasure, he has been more nearly correct than the official force."

"Oh, if you say so, Mr. Jones, it is all right," said the stranger. "Still, I confess that I miss my rubber. It is the first Sunday night for seven-and-twenty years that I have not had my rubber."

"I think you will find," said Sherlock Holmes, "that you will play for a higher stake to-night than you have ever done yet, and that the play will be more exciting. For you, Sir John, the stake will be some £3,000,000; and for you, Jones, it will be a man upon whom you wish to lay your hands. Adolph Mayer, of 13 Great George Street, Westminster, the murderer, thief, spy, and forger. He is a young man, Sir John, but he is at the head of his profession."

"I would rather have my bracelets on him than on any criminal in London," said Jones.

"He is a remarkable man, is young Adolph Mayer. His grandfather was a German royal duke, and he himself has been to the Humboldtian University of Berlin as well as Eton and Oxford. His brain is as cunning as his fingers, and though we meet signs of him at every turn, we never know where to find the man himself. He will crack a crib in Scotland one week, and be raising money to build an orphanage in Munich the next. I have been on his track for years and have set eyes on him only recently."

"I hope that I may have the pleasure of introducing you to-night. I've had one or two little turns also with Mr. Adolph Mayer, and I agree with you that he is at the head of his profession," said Jones.

Sherlock Holmes was not communicative during the rest of the long drive and lay back in the cab humming the tunes which he had heard in the afternoon. We rattled through an endless labyrinth of gas-lit streets until we emerged into Horse Guards Road.

"We are close there now," my friend remarked. "I apologise Sir John, I have not yet formally introduced you to Dr. Watson, my friend and long-time colleague. This Watson, is Sir John Simon, Attorney General of Great Brittan and the chief legal adviser of the Crown and its government. He provides legal advice to the Government and acts as the representative of the public interest in this matter. I thought it as well to have Jones with us also. He is as brave as a bulldog and as tenacious as a lobster if he gets his claws upon anyone. Here we are."

We had reached the same crowded thoroughfare in which we had found ourselves in earlier. Our cab was dismissed, and, following the guidance of Sir John, we ran the gauntlet of the guards and passed into the back, down a narrow passage and through a side door, which he opened for us. Within there was a small corridor, which ended in a massive iron gate. This also was opened, and led down a flight of winding stone steps, which terminated at another formidable gate. Sir John stopped to light a lantern, and then conducted us down a dark, earth-smelling passage, and so, after opening a third door, into a huge vault or cellar, which was piled all round with crates and massive boxes.

"You are not very vulnerable from above," Holmes remarked as he held up the lantern and gazed about him.

"Nor from below," said Sir John, striking his stick upon the flags which lined the floor. "Why, dear me, it sounds quite hollow!" he remarked, looking up in surprise.

"I must really ask you to be a little more quiet!" said Holmes severely. "You have already imperilled the whole success of our expedition. Might I beg that you would have the goodness to sit down upon one of those boxes, and not to interfere?"

The solemn Sir John perched himself upon a crate, with an injured expression upon his face, while Holmes fell upon his knees upon the floor and, with the lantern and a magnifying lens, began to examine minutely the cracks between the stones. A few seconds sufficed to satisfy him, for he sprang to his feet again and put his glass in his pocket.

"We have some wait before us," he remarked, "for they can hardly take any steps until the quiet hours of the night. Then they will not lose a minute, for the sooner they do their work the longer time they will have for their escape. We are at present, Doctor—as no doubt you have divined—in the secure vaults in the basements of 10 Downing Street, and it should be obvious to you that there are reasons why the more daring criminals of Europe should take a considerable interest in this cellar at present."

Holmes was cold and stern and silent. As the gleam of the lamp fell upon his austere features, I saw that his brows were drawn down in thought and his thin lips compressed. I knew not what wild beast we were about to hunt down in the dark jungle of criminal London, but I was well assured, from the bearing of this master huntsman, that the adventure was a most grave one—while the sardonic smile which occasionally broke through his ascetic gloom boded little good for the object of our quest.

"And now it is time that we arranged our little plans. I expect that within an hour matters will come to a head. In the meantime Sir John, we must put the screen over that dark lantern."

"And sit in the dark?"

"I am afraid so. I had brought a pack of cards in my pocket, and I thought that, as we were a *partie carrée*, you might have your rubber after all. But I see that the enemy's preparations have gone so far that we cannot risk the presence of a light. And, first of all, we must choose our positions. These are daring men, and though we shall take them at a disadvantage, they may do us some harm unless we are careful. I shall stand behind this crate, and do you conceal yourselves behind those. Then, when I flash a light upon them, close in swiftly. If they fire, Watson, have no compunction about shooting them down."

I placed my revolver, cocked, upon the top of the wooden case behind which I crouched. Holmes shot the slide across the front of his lantern and left us in pitch darkness—such an absolute darkness as I have never before experienced. The smell of hot metal remained to assure us that the light was still there, ready to flash out at a moment's notice. To me, with my nerves worked up to a pitch of expectancy, there was something depressing and subduing in the sudden gloom, and in the cold dank air of the vault.

"They have but one retreat," whispered Holmes. "That is back through the tunnel into the Park Offices. I hope that you have done what I asked you, Jones?"

"I have an inspector and two officers waiting at the front door."

"Then we have stopped all the holes. And now we must be silent and wait."

What a time it seemed! From comparing notes afterwards it was but an hour and a quarter, yet it appeared to me that the night must have almost gone, and the dawn be breaking above us. My limbs were weary and stiff, for I feared to change my position; yet my nerves were worked up to the highest pitch of tension, and my hearing was so acute that I could not only hear the gentle breathing of my companions, but I could distinguish the deeper, heavier in-breath of the bulky Jones from the thin, sighing note of the Attorney General. From my position I could look over the case in the direction of the floor. Suddenly my eyes caught the glint of a light.

At first it was but a lurid spark upon the stone pavement. Then it lengthened out until it became a yellow line, and then, without any warning or sound, a gash seemed to open and a hand appeared, a white, almost womanly hand, which felt about in the centre of the little area of light. For a minute or more the hand, with its writhing fingers, protruded out of the floor. Then it was withdrawn as suddenly as it appeared, and all was dark again save the single lurid spark which marked a chink between the stones.

Its disappearance, however, was but momentary. With a rending, tearing sound, one of the broad, white stones turned over upon its side and left a square, gaping hole, through which streamed the light of a lantern. Over the edge there peeped a clean-cut, boyish face, which looked keenly about it, and then, with a hand on either side of the aperture, drew itself shoulder-high and waist-high, until one knee rested upon the edge. In another instant he stood at the side of the hole and was hauling after him a companion, lithe and small like himself, with a pale face and a shock of very red hair.

"It is all clear," he whispered. "Have you the chisel and the bags? Donnerwetter! Jump, Louis, jump, and I vill--"

Sherlock Holmes had sprung out and seized the intruder by the collar. The other dived down the hole, and I heard the sound of rending cloth as Jones clutched at his shirts. The light flashed upon the barrel of a revolver, but Holmes' hunting crop came down on the man's wrist, and the pistol clinked upon the stone floor.

"It is no use, Adolph Mayer," said Holmes blandly. "You have no chance at all."

"So I see," the other answered with the utmost coolness. "I fancy that my colleague is all right, though I see you have got his coat-tails."

"There are three men waiting for him at the door," said Holmes.

"Oh, indeed! You seem to have done the thing completely. I must compliment you."

"And I you," Holmes answered. "Your idea was new and effective."

"You'll see your pal again presently," said Jones. "He's quicker at climbing down holes than I am. Just hold out while I fix the derbies."

"I beg that you will not touch me with your filthy hands," remarked our prisoner as the handcuffs clattered upon his wrists. "You may not be aware that I have royal blood in my veins. Have the goodness, also, when you address me always to say 'sir' and 'please.'"

"All right," said Jones with a stare and a snigger. "Well, would you please, Sir, march upstairs, where we can get a cab to carry your Highness to the police-station?"

"That is better," said Adolph Mayer serenely. He made a sweeping bow to the three of us and walked quietly off in the custody of the detective.

"Really, Mr. Holmes," said Sir John as we followed them from the cellar, "I do not know how we can thank you or repay you. There is no doubt that you have detected and defeated in the most complete manner one of the most determined attempts at robbery that have ever come within my experience."

"I have had one or two little scores of my own to settle with Mr. Adolph Mayer," said Holmes, "and I am amply repaid by having had an experience which is in many ways unique."

"You see, Watson," he explained in the early hours of the morning as we sat over a glass of whisky and soda in Baker Street, "it was perfectly obvious from our first warning that an attempt would be made on our gold reserves held at # 10 Downing Street. The question was how and when? As to how, I started by visiting the area several times and considered how an attempt on it could be made. First, its surroundings: Number 10 is bordered by the buildings of Parliament and government office on three sides. On the forth, is St. James Park. An assault was always a possibility. However, given the constant military and police presence in the area, I considered that to be unlikely. An inside job had also to be considered, but Petrovic's warning did not mention watching an individual but watching the gold. As we were riding the underground to Westminster, I cast my mind to the clay kickers who constructed the Twopenny Tube. A tunnel under #10, directly into the vaults where the gold is kept, then suggested itself to me as a possibility. The tunnel, I considered, must have a starting place and would necessitate the movement of large amounts of dirt and debris. I immediately recalled the extensive gardens and earth-works I had seen surrounding the little cottages in St. James Park. When I returned to the area, I found that those were the park offices and, indeed, they were the closest non-government unsecured buildings to #10. Further researches revealed that the front office was only occupied from 6am until 3pm, the gardeners and tradesmen there preferring an early shift, and the residence being in the back building. That left the place empty for many hours a day. We then went round to meet some of the inhabitants and you know what took place then. As to when, by the advanced state of their preparations and by calculating the volume of dirt that had to be removed to make a 250 yard tunnel, I surmised that tonight, which had the advantages of being a Sunday night – the quietest night of the week, would be the night they struck."

Chapter 6: Irene Adler's tale

"I should certainly do it," said Sherlock Holmes.

I started at the interruption, for my companion had been eating his breakfast with his attention entirely centred upon the paper which was propped up by the coffee pot. Now I looked across at him to find his eyes fastened upon me with the half-amused, half-questioning expression which he usually assumed when he felt that he had made an intellectual point.

"Do what?" I asked.

He smiled as he took his slipper from the mantelpiece and drew from it enough shag tobacco to fill the old clay pipe with which he invariably rounded off his breakfast.

"A most characteristic question of yours, Watson," he said. "You will not, I am sure, be offended if I say that any reputation for sharpness which I may possess has been entirely gained by the admirable foil which you have made for me. Have I not heard of debutantes who have insisted upon plainness in their chaperones? There is a certain analogy."

Our long companionship in the Baker Street rooms had left us on those easy terms of intimacy when much may be said without offense. And yet I knowledge that I was nettled at his remark.

"I may be very obtuse," said I, "but I confess that I am unable to see how you have managed to know that I was ... I was ..."

"Asked to help in the Edinburgh University Bazaar."

"Precisely. The letter has only just come to hand, and I have not spoken to you since."

"In spite of that," said Holmes, leaning back in his chair and putting his fingertips together, "I would even venture to suggest that the object of the bazaar is to enlarge the University cricket field."

I looked at him in such bewilderment that he vibrated with silent laughter.

"The fact is, my dear Watson, that you are an excellent subject," said he. "You are never blasé. You respond instantly to any external stimulus. Your mental processes may be slow but they are never obscure, and I found during breakfast that you were easier reading than the leader in the *Times* in front of me."

"I should be glad to know how you arrived at your conclusions," said I.

"I fear that my good nature in giving explanations has seriously compromised my reputation," said Holmes. "But in this case the train of reasoning is based upon such obvious facts that no credit can be claimed for it. You entered the room with a thoughtful expression, the expression of a man who was debating some point in his mind. In your hand you held a solitary letter. Now last night you retired in the best of spirits, so it was clear that it was this letter in your hand which had caused the change in you."

"This is obvious."

"It is all obvious when it is explained to you. I naturally asked myself what the letter could contain which might have this effect upon you. As you walked you held the flap side of the envelope towards me, and I saw upon it the same shield-shaped device which I have observed upon your old college cricket cap. It was clear, then, that the request came from Edinburgh University - or from some club connected with the University. When you reached the table you lay down the letter beside your plate with the address uppermost, and you walked over to look at the framed photograph upon the left of the mantelpiece."

It amazed me to see the accuracy with which he had observed my movements. "What next?" I asked.

"I began by glancing at the address, and I can tell, even at the distance of six feet, that it was an unofficial communication. This I gathered from the use of the word 'Doctor' upon the address, to which, as a Bachelor of Medicine, you have no legal claim. I knew that University officials are pedantic in their correct use of titles, and I was thus enabled to say with certainty that your letter was unofficial. When on your return to the table you turned over your letter and allowed me to perceive that the enclosure was a printed one, the idea of a bazaar first occurred to me. I had already weighed the possibility of its being a political communication, but this seemed improbable in the present stagnant conditions of politics.

"When you returned to the table your face still retained its expression and it was evident that your examination of the photograph had not changed the current of your thoughts. In that case it must itself bear upon the subject in question. I turned my attention to the photograph, therefore, and saw at once that it consisted of yourself as a member of the Edinburgh University Eleven, with the pavilion and cricket-field in the background. My small experience of cricket clubs has taught me that next to churches and cavalry ensigns they are the most debt-laden things upon earth. When upon your return to the table I saw you take out your pencil and draw lines upon the envelope, I was convinced that you were endeavouring to realize some projected improvement which was to be brought about by a bazaar. Your face still showed some indecision, so that I was able to break in upon you with my advice that you should assist in so good an object."

I could not help smiling at the extreme simplicity of his explanation. "Of course, it was as easy as possible. It is simple enough as you explain it," I said, smiling. "You remind me of Edgar Allen Poe's Dupin."

Sherlock Holmes rose and lit his pipe. "No doubt you think that you are complimenting me in comparing me to Dupin," he observed. "Now, in my opinion, Dupin was a very inferior fellow. That trick of his of breaking in on his friends' thoughts with an apropos remark after a quarter of an hour's silence is really very showy and superficial. He had some analytical genius, no doubt; but he was by no means such a phenomenon as Poe appeared to imagine."

"Have you read Gaboriau's works?" I asked. "Does Lecoq come up to your idea of a detective?"
Sherlock Holmes sniffed sardonically. "Lecoq was a miserable bungler," he said, in an angry voice; "he had only one thing to recommend him, and that was his energy. That book made me positively ill. The question was how to identify an unknown prisoner. I could have done it in twenty-four hours. Lecoq took six months or so. It might be made a text-book for detectives to teach them what to avoid."

I felt rather indignant at having two characters whom I had admired treated in this cavalier style. I walked over to the window, and stood looking out into the busy street.

"I may add," said he, "that the particular help which you have been asked to give was that you should write in their album, and that you have already made up your mind that the present incident will be the subject of your article."

"But how -!" I cried.

"It is as easy as possible," said he, "and I leave its solution to your own ingenuity. In the meantime," he added, raising the paper, "you will excuse me if I return to this very interesting article upon the trees of Cremona, and the exact reasons for their pre-eminence in the manufacture of violins. It is one of those small outlying problems to which I am sometimes tempted to direct my attention."

"I trust," said I, a while later after breakfast, "that you are satisfied with our recent activities. But you look weary."

"Yes, the reaction is already upon me. I shall be as limp as a rag for a week."

"Strange," said I, "how terms of what in another man I should call laziness alternate with your fits of splendid energy and vigour."

"Yes," he answered, "there are in me the makings of a fine loafer and also of a pretty spry sort of fellow. I often think of those lines of old Goethe,—

> Schade dass die Natur nur einen Mensch aus Dir schuf, Denn zum wuerdigen Mann war und zum Schelmen der Stoff."

An anomaly which often struck me in the character of my friend Sherlock Holmes was that, although in his methods of thought he was the neatest and most methodical of mankind, and although also he affected a certain quiet primness of dress, he was none the less in his personal habits one of the most untidy men that ever drove a fellow-lodger to distraction. Not that I am in the least conventional in that respect myself. The rough-and-tumble of my early work in Afghanistan, coming on the top of a natural Bohemianism of disposition, has made me rather more lax than befits a medical man. But with me there is a limit, and when I find a man who keeps his cigars in the coal-scuttle, his tobacco in the toe end of a Persian slipper, and his unanswered correspondence transfixed by a jack-knife into the very centre of his wooden mantelpiece, then I begin to give myself virtuous airs. I have always held, too, that pistol practice should be distinctly an open-air pastime; and when Holmes, in one of his queer humours, would sit in an arm-chair with his hair-trigger and a hundred Boxer cartridges, and proceed to adorn the opposite wall with a patriotic V. R. done in bullet-pocks, I felt strongly that neither the atmosphere nor the appearance of our room was improved by it.

Our chambers were always full of chemicals and of criminal relics which had a way of wandering into unlikely positions, and of turning up in the butter-dish or in even less desirable places. But his papers were my great crux. He had a horror of destroying documents, especially those which were connected with his past cases, and yet it was only once in every year or two that he would muster energy to docket and arrange them; for, as I have mentioned somewhere in these incoherent memoirs, the outbursts of passionate energy when he performed the remarkable feats with which his name is associated were followed by reactions of lethargy during which he would lie about with his violin and his books, hardly moving save from the sofa to the table.

Even the triumphant issue of his labours could not always save him from reaction after an exertion. Now, at a time when Europe was creeping toward war and he was powerless to stop it, I found him a prey to the blackest depression. Even the knowledge that he had succeeded in foiling the theft of the gold reserves, was insufficient to rouse him from his nervous prostration.

Sherlock Holmes took his bottle from the corner of the mantel-piece and his hypodermic syringe from its neat morocco case. With his long, white, nervous fingers he adjusted the delicate needle, and rolled back his left shirt-cuff. For some little time his eyes rested thoughtfully upon the sinewy forearm and wrist all dotted and scarred with innumerable puncture-marks. Finally he thrust the sharp point home, pressed down the tiny piston, and sank back into the velvet-lined arm-chair with a long sigh of satisfaction.

Too many times I had witnessed this performance, but custom had not reconciled my mind to it. On the contrary, I had become more irritable at the sight, and my conscience swelled within me at the thought that I had lacked the courage to protest. Again and again I had registered a vow that I should deliver my soul upon the subject, but there was that in the cool, nonchalant air of my companion which made him the last man with whom one would care to take anything approaching to a liberty. His great powers, his masterly manner, and the experience which I had had of his many extraordinary qualities, all made me diffident and backward in crossing him.

Yet upon that morning, whether it was the Strengthening Jelly which I had taken with my breakfast, or the additional exasperation produced by the extreme deliberation of his manner, I suddenly felt that I could hold out no longer.

"Which is it to-day?" I asked,—"morphine or cocaine?"

He raised his eyes languidly from the old black-letter volume which he had opened. "It is cocaine," he said,—"a seven-per-cent solution. Would you care to try it?"

"No, indeed," I answered, brusquely.

He smiled at my vehemence. "Perhaps you are right, Watson," he said. "I suppose that its influence is physically a bad one. I find it, however, so transcendently stimulating and clarifying to the mind that its secondary action is a matter of small moment."

"But consider!" I said, earnestly. "Count the cost! Your brain may, as you say, be roused and excited, but it is a pathological and morbid process, which involves increased tissue-change and may at last leave a permanent weakness. You know, too, what a black reaction comes upon you. Surely the game is hardly worth the candle. Why should you, for a mere passing pleasure, risk the loss of those great powers with which you have been endowed? Remember that I speak not only as one comrade to another, but as a medical man to one for whose constitution he is to some extent answerable."

He did not seem offended. On the contrary, he put his finger-tips together and leaned his elbows on the arms of his chair, like one who has a relish for conversation.

"My mind," he said, "rebels at stagnation. Give me problems, give me work, give me the most abstruse cryptogram or the most intricate analysis, and I am in my own proper atmosphere. I can dispense then with artificial stimulants. But I abhor the dull routine of existence. I crave for mental exaltation. That is, as you know, why I have chosen – created – my own particular profession."

After a while, filling up his old brier-root pipe, he said, "I was consulted last week by Chevalier C. Auguste Dupin, who, as you probably know, has come rather to the attention lately of the French detective service for his handling of the Larrabee case at that end. He has all the Celtic power of quick intuition, but he is deficient in the wide range of exact knowledge which is essential to the higher developments of his art. The case was concerned with a letter, and possessed some features of interest. I was able to refer him to two parallel cases, the one at Riga in 1857, and the other at St. Louis in 1871, which have suggested to him the true solution. Here is the letter which I had this morning acknowledging my assistance." He tossed over, as he spoke, a crumpled sheet of foreign notepaper. I glanced my eyes down it, catching a profusion of notes of admiration, with stray "magnifiques," "coup-de-maitres," and "tours-de-force," all testifying to the ardent admiration of the Frenchman.

"He speaks as a pupil to his master," said I.

"Oh, he rates my assistance too highly," said Sherlock Holmes, lightly. "He has considerable gifts himself. He possesses two out of the three qualities necessary for the ideal detective. He has the power of observation and that of deduction. He is only wanting in knowledge; and that may come in time. He has finally finished translating my small works into French."

"Your works?"

"Oh, do you not recall?" he cried, laughing. "Yes, I have been guilty of several monographs. They are all upon technical subjects. Here, for example, is one 'Upon the Distinction between the Ashes of the Various Tobaccoes.' In it I enumerate a hundred and forty forms of cigar-, cigarette-, and pipe-tobacco, with coloured plates illustrating the difference in the ash. It is a point which is continually turning up in criminal trials, and which is sometimes of supreme importance as a clue. If you can say definitely, for example, that some murder has been done by a man who was smoking an Indian lunkah, it obviously narrows your field of search. To the trained eye there is as much difference between the black ash of a Trichinopoly and the white fluff of bird's-eye as there is between a cabbage and a potato."

"You have always had an extraordinary genius for minutiae," I remarked.

"I appreciate their importance. Here is my monograph upon the tracing of footsteps, with some remarks upon the uses of plaster of Paris as a preserver of impresses. Here, too, is a curious little work upon the influence of a trade upon the form of the hand, with lithotypes of the hands of slaters, sailors, corkcutters, compositors, weavers, and diamond-polishers. That is a matter of great practical interest to the scientific detective,—especially in cases of unclaimed bodies, or in discovering the antecedents of criminals. But I weary you with my hobby."

"Not at all," I answered, earnestly. "It is of the greatest interest to me, especially since I have had the opportunity of observing and chronicling your practical application of it. But you spoke just now of observation and deduction. Surely the one to some extent implies the other."

"Why, hardly," he answered, leaning back luxuriously in his arm-chair, and sending up thick blue wreaths from his pipe. "For example, observation shows me that you have been to the Wigmore Street Post-Office this morning, but deduction lets me know that when there you dispatched a telegram."

"Right!" said I. "Right on both points! But I confess that I do not see how you arrived at it. It was a sudden impulse upon my part, and I have mentioned it to no one."

"It is simplicity itself," he remarked, chuckling at my surprise,—"so absurdly simple that an explanation is superfluous; and yet it may serve to define the limits of observation and of deduction. Observation tells me that you have a little reddish mould adhering to your instep. Just opposite the Seymour Street Office they have taken up the pavement and thrown up some earth which lies in such a way that it is difficult to avoid treading in it in entering. The earth is of this peculiar reddish tint which is found, as far as I know, nowhere else in the neighbourhood. So much is observation. The rest is deduction."

"How, then, did you deduce the telegram?"

"Why, of course I knew that you had not written a letter, since I sat opposite to you all morning. I see also in your open desk there that you have a sheet of stamps and a thick bundle of post-cards. What could you go into the post-office for, then, but to send a wire? Eliminate all other factors, and the one which remains must be the truth."

"In this case it certainly is so," I replied, after a little thought. I could not help laughing at the ease with which he explained his process of deduction. "When I hear you give your reasons," I remarked, "the thing always appears to me to be so ridiculously simple that I could easily do it myself, though at each successive instance of your reasoning I am baffled until you explain your process. And yet I believe that my eyes are as good as yours."

"Quite so," he answered, lighting a cigarette, and throwing himself down into an armchair. "You see, but you do not observe. The distinction is clear. For example, you have frequently seen the steps which lead up from the hall to this room."

"Frequently."

"How often?"

"Well, many hundreds of times."

"Then how many are there?"

"How many? I do not know."

"Quite so! You have not observed. And yet you have seen. That is just my point. Now, I know that there are seventeen steps, simply because I have both seen and observed."

"The thing, however, is, as you say, of the simplest. Would you think me impertinent if I were to put your theories to a more severe test?"

"On the contrary," he answered, "it would prevent me from taking a second dose of cocaine. I should be delighted to look into any problem which you might submit to me."

"I have heard you say that it is difficult for a man to have any object in daily use without leaving the impress of his individuality upon it in such a way that a trained observer might read it. Now, I have here a watch which has recently come into my possession. Would you have the kindness to let me have an opinion upon the character or habits of the late owner?"

I handed him over the watch with some slight feeling of amusement in my heart, for the test was, as I thought, an impossible one, and I intended it as a lesson against the somewhat dogmatic tone which he occasionally assumed. He balanced the watch in his hand, gazed hard at the dial, opened the back, and examined the works, first with his naked eyes and then with a powerful convex lens. I could hardly keep from smiling at his crestfallen face when he finally snapped the case to and handed it back.

"There are hardly any data," he remarked. "The watch has been recently cleaned, which robs me of my most suggestive facts."

"You are right," I answered. "It was cleaned before being sent to me." In my heart I accused my companion of putting forward a most lame and impotent excuse to cover his failure. What data could he expect from an uncleaned watch?

"Though unsatisfactory, my research has not been entirely barren," he observed, staring up at the ceiling with dreamy, lack-lustre eyes. "Subject to your correction, I should judge that the watch belonged to your elder brother, who inherited it from your father."

"That you gather, no doubt, from the H. W. upon the back?"

"Quite so. The W. suggests your own name. The date of the watch is nearly fifty years back, and the initials are as old as the watch: so it was made for the last generation. Jewellery usually descends to the eldest son, and he is most likely to have the same name as the father. Your father has, if I remember right, been dead many years. It has, therefore, been in the hands of your eldest brother."

"Right, so far," said I. "Anything else?"

"He was a man of untidy habits,—very untidy and careless. He was left with good prospects, but he threw away his chances, lived for some time in poverty with occasional short intervals of prosperity, and finally, taking to drink, he died. That is all I can gather."

I sprang from my chair and walked impatiently about the room with considerable bitterness in my heart.

"This is unworthy of you, Holmes," I said. "I could not have believed that you would have descended to this. You have made inquires into the history of my unhappy brother, and you now pretend to deduce this knowledge in some fanciful way. You cannot expect me to believe that you have read all this from his old watch! It is unkind, and, to speak plainly, has a touch of charlatanism in it."

"My dear doctor," said he, kindly, "pray accept my apologies. Viewing the matter as an abstract problem, I had forgotten how personal and painful a thing it might be to you. I assure you, however, that I never even knew that you had a brother until you handed me the watch."

"Then how in the name of all that is wonderful did you get these facts? They are absolutely correct in every particular."

"Ah, that is good luck. I could only say what was the balance of probability. I did not at all expect to be so accurate."

"But it was not mere guess-work?"

"No, no: I never guess. It is a shocking habit,—destructive to the logical faculty. What seems strange to you is only so because you do not follow my train of thought or observe the small facts upon which large inferences may depend. For example, I began by stating that your brother was careless. When you observe the lower part of that watch-case you notice that it is not only dinted in two places, but it is cut and marked all over from the habit of keeping other hard objects, such as coins or keys, in the same pocket. Surely it is no great feat to assume that a man who treats a fifty-guinea watch so cavalierly must be a careless man. Neither is it a far-fetched inference that a man who inherits one article of such value is pretty well provided for in other respects."

I nodded, to show that I followed his reasoning.

"It is customary for pawnbrokers in England, when they take a watch, to scratch the number of the ticket with a pin-point upon the inside of the case. It is more handy than a label, as there is no risk of the number being lost or transposed. There are no less than four such numbers visible to my lens on the inside of this case. Inference,—that your brother was often at low water. Secondary inference,—that he had occasional bursts of prosperity, or he could not have redeemed the pledge. Finally, I ask you to look at the inner plate, which contains the key-hole. Look at the thousands of scratches all round the hole,—marks where the key has slipped. What sober man's key could have scored those grooves? But you will never see a drunkard's watch without them. He winds it at night, and he leaves these traces of his unsteady hand. Where is the mystery in all this?"

"It is as clear as daylight," I answered. "I regret the injustice which I did you. I should have had more faith in your marvellous faculty."

"I cannot live without brain-work. What else is there to live for? Stand at the window here. Was ever such a dreary, dismal, unprofitable world? See how the yellow fog swirls down the street and drifts across the dun-coloured houses. What could be more hopelessly prosaic and material? What is the use of having powers, doctor, when one has no field upon which to exert them? Crime is commonplace, existence is commonplace, and no qualities save those which are commonplace have any function upon earth."

Later that day, after I had succeeded in rousing Holmes and we had gone out for one of our afternoon rambles, we returned about six o'clock. As Holmes turned up the lamp the light fell upon a card on the table. He glanced at it, and then, with an ejaculation he turned it over and handed it to me:

IRENE NORTON, *née* ADLER.

"Not Irene Adler?" I cried, in amazement. "I thought she had gone to the continent never to return?"

"The woman has returned," Holmes answered, as he sat down and stretched his legs. "I asked her to come here to explain what has happened to James Larrabee and what it was that she took from him."

I turned the card over. "Will call at 6:30," I read.

"Hum! She is about due."

To Sherlock Holmes she is always *the* woman. I have seldom heard him mention her under any other name. She has a soul of steel, the face of the most beautiful of women, and the mind of the most resolute of men. In his eyes she eclipses and predominates the whole of her sex. It was not that he felt any emotion akin to love for Irene Adler. All emotions, and that one particularly, were abhorrent to his cold, precise but admirably balanced mind. He was, I take it, the most perfect reasoning and observing machine that the world has seen, but as a lover he would have placed himself in a false position. He never spoke of the softer passions, save with a gibe and a sneer. They were admirable things for the observer—excellent for drawing the veil from men's motives and actions. But for the trained reasoner to admit such intrusions into his own delicate and finely adjusted temperament was to introduce a distracting factor which might throw a doubt upon all his mental results. Grit in a sensitive instrument, or a crack in one of his own high-power lenses, would not be more disturbing than a strong emotion in a nature such as his. And yet there was but one woman to him, and that woman was Irene Adler, of dubious and questionable memory.

At that instant there was a clatter and a rattle in the street below. Looking down I saw a stately carriage and pair, the brilliant lamps gleaming on the glossy haunches of the noble chestnuts. A footman opened the door, and she emerged. Irene Adler, as I will still call her, stood at the top with her superb figure outlined against the lights of the carriage, looking back into the street. She was a lovely woman, with a face that a man might die for. A minute later she was in the room. Our modest apartment, distinguished over the years by Royalty and Ministers alike, was further honoured by the entrance of the most lovely woman in London. No description of it, and no contemplation of colourless photographs, had prepared me for the subtle, delicate charm and the beautiful colouring of that exquisite head.

She swept across the room and seated herself with her back to the window. It was a queenly presence—tall, graceful, and intensely womanly. "My dear Mr. Sherlock Holmes, Dr. Watson. I had your note and I will get right to the point and I will tell you what you want to know. Do you feel a creeping, shrinking sensation, when you stand before the serpents in the Zoo, and see the slithery, gliding, venomous creatures, with their deadly eyes and wicked, flattened faces? Well, that is how James Larrabee impresses, or shall I say impressed, me. I have had to do with many types of people in my career, but the worst of them never gave me the repulsion which I had for this fellow. And yet I could not get out of doing business with him."

"Pray continue," said Holmes.

"He was the king of all the blackmailers. Heaven help the man, and still more the woman, whose secret and reputation came into the power of James Larrabee! With a smiling face and a heart of marble, he would squeeze and squeeze until he had drained them dry. The fellow was a genius in his way, and would have made his mark in some more savoury trade. His method was as follows: He allowed it to be known that he was prepared to pay very high sums for letters which compromised people of wealth and position. He received these wares not only from treacherous valets or maids, but frequently from genteel ruffians, who have gained the confidence and affection of trusting women. He paid well for his information. I happen to know that he paid seven hundred pounds to a footman for a note two lines in length, and that the ruin of a noble family was the result. Everything which is in the market went to James Larrabee, and there are hundreds in this great city who turn white at his name. No one knows where his grip may fall, for he is far too rich and far too cunning to work from hand to mouth. He will hold a card back for years in order to play it at the moment when the stake is best worth winning. I have said that he was the worst man in London, and I would ask you how could one compare the ruffian, who in hot blood bludgeons his mate, with this man, who methodically and at his leisure tortured the soul and wrung the nerves in order to add to his already swollen money-bags?"

I had seldom heard anyone speak with such intensity of feeling. "But surely," said I, "the fellow must have been within the grasp of the law?"

"Technically, no doubt, but practically not. What would it profit a woman, for example, to get him a few months' imprisonment if her own ruin must immediately follow? His victims dare not hit back. If ever he blackmailed an innocent person, then indeed the police should have him, but he was as cunning as the Evil One. No, no, I had to find other ways to fight him."

"And why was that?" asked Holmes.

"Because an illustrious lady, a long-time friend of mine, had placed her piteous case in my hands. The lady, the most beautiful debutante of last season, is to be married in a fortnight to the Earl of Dovercourt. This fiend Larrabee had several imprudent letters—imprudent, nothing worse—which were written to an impecunious young squire in the country.

They would suffice to break off the match. Larrabee threatened to send the letters to the Earl unless a large sum of money was paid him. I was asked, as a woman of the world, to meet him, and—to make the best terms I could."

"You met Larrabee at Godolphin Street. What happened there, madam?"

"I tapped at the door as agreed. Larrabee opened it. I followed him into his room, leaving the hall door ajar behind me, for an easier retreat. I remember that there was a woman outside as I entered. Our business was soon done. He had the letters on his desk, I handed him the money. He gave me the letters. At this instant there was a sound at the door. There were steps in the passage. Larrabee quickly turned back the drugget, thrust the money into some hiding-place there, and covered it over.

"What happened after that is like some dream. I have a vision of a dark, frantic face, of a woman's voice, which screamed in French, 'My waiting is not in vain. At last, at last I have found you with her!' There was a savage struggle. I saw him with a chair in his hand, a knife gleamed in hers. I rushed from the scene, ran from the house, and only next morning in the paper did I learn the dreadful result. That night I was happy, for I had the letters, and I had not seen yet my opportunity to regain the money as well.

"It was the next morning that I realised that the money must still be where Larrabee had placed it, for it was concealed before this dreadful woman entered the room. If it had not been for her coming, I should not have known where his hiding-place was. How was I to get into the room? For two days I watched the place, but the door was never left open. That night I made my attempt. What I did and how I succeeded, you have obviously already learned."

Her story at an end, she rose and walked across the room. She looked back at us from the door, and I had a last impression of that beautiful face. Then she was gone.

"I think she is the most remarkable lady I ever met, and might have been most useful in such work as we have been doing. She has a decided genius that way: witness the way in which she preserved the money and the letter. But love is an emotional thing, and whatever is emotional is opposed to that true cold reason which I place above all things. I should never marry myself, lest I bias my judgment."

Chapter 7: Epilogue

It was pleasant for Dr. Watson to find himself that afternoon as usual in the untidy room of the first floor in Baker Street which he had for so long shared with his friend Sherlock Holmes. He looked round him at the scientific charts upon the wall, the acid-charred bench of chemicals, the violin-case leaning in the corner, the coal-scuttle, which contained the pipes and tobacco. Finally, his eyes came round to the fresh and smiling face of Billy, the young but wise and tactful page, who often helped a little to fill up the gap which surrounded the saturnine figure of the great detective.

Billy glanced with some solicitude at the closed door of the bedroom.

"I think he's in bed and asleep," he said.

It was seven in the evening of a lovely summer's day, but Dr. Watson was sufficiently familiar with the irregularity of his old friend's hours to feel no surprise at the idea.

"He's following someone." he continued. "Yesterday he was out as a workman looking for a job. The day before he was an old Irishman with a goatee beard. To-day he was an old woman. Fairly took me in, he did, and I ought to know his ways by now." Billy pointed with a grin to a baggy parasol which leaned against the sofa. "That's part of the old woman's outfit," he said.

"I say, Billy, what is that curtain for across the window?" ask Dr. Watson.

"Mr. Holmes had it put up there this morning after you left. We've got something funny behind it."
Billy advanced and drew away the drapery which screened the alcove of the bow window.

Dr. Watson could not restrain a cry of amazement. There was a facsimile of his friend, dressing-gown and all, the face turned three-quarters towards the window and downward,

109

as though reading an invisible book, while the body was sunk deep in an armchair. Billy detached the head and held it in the air.

"I am to put it at different angles, so that it may seem more lifelike. I wouldn't dare touch it if the blind were not down. But when it's up you can see this from across the way."

"We used something of the sort before."

"Before my time," said Billy. He drew the window curtains apart and looked out into the street. "There are folk who watch us from over yonder. I can see a fellow now at the window. Have a look for yourself."

Watson had taken a step forward when the bedroom door opened, and the long, thin form of Holmes emerged, his face pale and drawn, but his step and bearing as active as ever. With a single spring he was at the window, and had drawn the blind once more.

"That will do, Billy," said he. "You were in danger of your life then, my boy, and I can not do without you just yet. Well, Watson, we have come to a critical moment."

"So I gather."

"You can go, Billy. That boy is a problem, Watson. How far am I justified in allowing him to be in danger?"

"Danger of what, Holmes?"

"Of sudden death. I'm expecting something this evening."

"Expecting what?"

"To be murdered, Watson."

"No, no, you are joking, Holmes!"

"Even my limited sense of humour could evolve a better joke than that. But we may be comfortable in the meantime, may we not? Is alcohol permitted? The gasogene and cigars are in their place. You have not, I hope, learned to despise my pipe and my lamentable tobacco? It has to take the place of food these days."

"But why not eat?"

"Because the faculties become refined when you starve them. Why, surely, as a doctor, my dear Watson, you must admit that what your digestion gains in the way of blood supply is so much lost to the brain. I am a brain, Watson. The rest of me is a mere appendix. Therefore, it is the brain I must consider."

"But this danger, Holmes?"

"Ah, yes, in case it should come off, it would perhaps be as well that you should burden your memory with the name and address of the murderer. You can give it to Scotland Yard, with my love and a parting blessing. Baron Von Herling is the name. Write it down, man, write it down! 136 Moorside Gardens, N. W. Got it?"

Watson's honest face was twitching with anxiety. He knew only too well the immense risks taken by Holmes and was well aware that what he said was more likely to be under-statement than exaggeration. Watson was always the man of action, and he rose to the occasion.

"Count me in, Holmes. I have nothing more important to do."

"Your morals do not improve, Watson. You have added fibbing to your other vices. You bear every sign of the busy medical man, with calls on him every hour."

"Not such important ones. But how do you know?"

"As to your practice, if a gentleman walks into my rooms smelling of iodoform, with a black mark of nitrate of silver upon his right forefinger, and a bulge on the right side of his top-hat to show where he has secreted his stethoscope, I must be dull, indeed, if I do not pronounce him to be an active member of the medical profession."

"Ah yes." replied Watson. "But you were speaking of this man, this Baron. Can you not have him arrested?"

"Yes, Watson, I could. That is what worries him so."

"But why don't you?"

"Because I want his confession. I have cast my net and I have my fish. But I have not got all the evidence I require and time is running out. We can make the world a better place by laying them by the heels."

"And is this Baron von Herling one of your fish?"

"Yes, and he is a shark. He bites. The other is Von Bork the sportsman. Not a bad fellow, Von Bork, but the Baron has used him. Von Bork is not a shark. He is a good sport and a hard-drinking, man-about-town ... a devil-may-care kind of fellow. But he is flopping about in my net all the same."

"Where is this Baron von Herling?"

"I have been at his very elbow all the morning. You have seen me as an old lady, Watson. I was never more convincing. He actually picked up my parasol for me once. 'By your leave, madame,' said he--German, you know, and with graces of manner when in the mood, but a devil incarnate in the other mood. Life is full of whimsical happenings, Watson."

"It might have been tragedy."

"Well, perhaps it might. I followed him to old Straubenzee's workshop in the Minories. Straubenzee made the air-gun--a very pretty bit of work, as I understand, and I rather fancy it is in the opposite window at the present moment. Have you seen the dummy? Of course, Billy showed it to you. Well, it may get a bullet through its beautiful head at any moment. Ah, Billy, what is it?"

The boy had reappeared in the room with a card upon a tray. Holmes glanced at it with raised eyebrows and an amused smile.

"The man himself. I had hardly expected this. Grasp the nettle, Watson! A man of nerve. Possibly you have heard of his reputation as a shooter of big game. It would indeed be a triumphant ending to his excellent sporting record if he added me to his bag. This is a proof that he feels my toe very close behind his heel."

"Send for the police."

"No police Watson. Would you glance carefully out of the window, and see if anyone is hanging about in the street?"

Watson looked warily round the edge of the curtain.

"No Holmes. The street is clear."

"Where is this gentleman, Billy?"

"In the waiting-room, sir."

"Show him up when I ring."

"Yes, sir."

"If I am not in the room, show him in all the same."

"Yes, sir."

Watson waited until the door was closed, and then he turned earnestly to his companion.

"Look here, Holmes, this is simply impossible. This is a desperate man, who sticks at nothing. He may have come to murder you."

"I should not be surprised."

"I insist upon staying with you."

"You would be horribly in the way."

"In his way?"

"No, my dear fellow--in my way."

"Well, I cannot possibly leave you."

"Yes, you can, Watson. And you will, for you have never failed to play the game. I am sure you will play it to the end. Come back in one hour Watson, and later, you can be my chauffer."

He touched the bell. "I think we will go out through the bedroom. This second exit is exceedingly useful. I rather want to see my shark without his seeing me, and I have, as you will remember, my own way of doing it."

It was, therefore, an empty room into which Billy, a minute later, ushered Baron von Herling. The famous game-shot was strong, fearless, and energetic, with a formidable dark moustache shading a cruel, thin-lipped mouth, and surmounted by a long, curved nose like the beak of an eagle. He was well dressed, but his brilliant necktie, shining pin, and glittering rings were flamboyant in their effect. As the door closed behind him he looked round him with fierce, startled eyes, like one who suspects a trap at every turn. Then he gave a violent start as he saw the impassive head and the collar of the dressing-gown which projected above the armchair in the window. At first his expression was one of pure amazement. Then the light of a horrible hope gleamed in his dark, murderous eyes. He took one more glance round to see that there were no witnesses, and then, on tiptoe, his thick stick half raised, he approached the silent figure. He was crouching for his final spring and blow when a cool, sardonic voice greeted him from the open bedroom door:

"Do not break it, Baron! Do not break it!"

The assassin staggered back, amazement in his convulsed face. For an instant he half raised his loaded cane once more, as if he would turn his violence from the effigy to the original; but there was something in that steady gray eye and mocking smile which caused his hand to sink to his side.

"It is a pretty little thing," said Holmes, advancing towards the image. "Tavernier, the French modeller, made it. He is as good at waxworks as your friend Straubenzee is at air-guns."

"Air-guns, sir! What do you mean?"

"Put your hat and stick on the side-table. Thank you! Pray take a seat. Would you care to put your revolver out also? Oh, very good, if you prefer to sit upon it. Your visit is really most opportune, for I wanted badly to have a few minutes' chat with you."

The Baron scowled, with heavy, threatening eyebrows.

"I, too, wished to have some words with you, Holmes. That is why I am here. I will not deny that I intended to assault you just now."

Holmes swung his leg on the edge of the table.

"I rather gathered that you had some idea of the sort in your head," said he. "But why these personal attentions?"

"Because you have gone out of your way to annoy me. Because you have put your creatures upon my track."

"My creatures! I assure you no!"

"Nonsense! I have had them followed. Two can play at that game, Holmes."

"It is a small point, Baron, but perhaps you would kindly give me my prefix when you address me. You can understand that, with my routine of work, I should find myself on familiar terms with half the rogues' gallery, and you will agree that exceptions are invidious."

"Well, Mr. Holmes, then."

"Excellent! But I assure you you are mistaken about my alleged agents."

Baron von Herling laughed contemptuously.

"Other people can observe as well as you. Yesterday there was an old sporting man. To-day it was an elderly woman. They held me in view all day."

"Really, sir, you compliment me. Old Baron Dowson said the night before he was hanged that in my case what the law had gained the stage had lost. And now you give my little impersonations your kindly praise?"

"It was you--you yourself?"

Holmes shrugged his shoulders. "You can see in the corner the parasol which you so politely handed to me in the Minories before you began to suspect."

"If I had known, you might never--"

"Have seen this humble home again. I was well aware of it. We all have neglected opportunities to deplore. As it happens, you did not know, so here we are!"

The Baron's knotted brows gathered more heavily over his menacing eyes. "What you say only makes the matter worse. It was not your agents but your play-acting, busybody self! You admit that you have dogged me. Why?"

"Come now, Count. You used to shoot lions in Algeria."

"Well?"

"But why?"

"Why? The sport--the excitement--the danger!"

"And, no doubt, to free the country from a pest?"

"Exactly!"

"My reasons in a nutshell!"

The Baron sprang to his feet, and his hand involuntarily moved back to his hip-pocket.

"Sit down, sir, sit down! There was another, more practical, reason. I want your confession!"

Baron von Herling lay back in his chair with an evil smile.

"Upon my word!" said he.

"You knew that I was after you. The real reason why you are here to-night is to find out how much I know about you and how far my removal is absolutely essential. Well, I should say that, from your point of view, it is absolutely essential, for I know all about you, save only one thing, which is how long you will spend in an English Goal."

"Oh, indeed?"

"You cannot bluff me, Baron." Holmes's eyes, as he gazed at him, contracted and lightened until they were like two menacing points of steel. "You are absolute plate-glass. I see to the very back of your mind."

"Then, of course, you see I have nothing to say!"

Holmes clapped his hands with amusement, and then pointed a derisive finger. "Now, Baron, if you will be reasonable we can do business. If not, you will get hurt."

Baron von Herling threw up his eyes to the ceiling. "And you talk about bluff!" said he.

Holmes looked at him thoughtfully like a master chess-player who meditates his crowning move. Then he threw open the table drawer and drew out a squat notebook.

"Do you know what I keep in this book?"

"No, sir, I do not!"

"You!"

"Me!"

"Yes, sir, you! You are all here--every action of your vile and dangerous life."

"Damn you, Holmes!" cried the Baron with blazing eyes. "There are limits to my patience!"

"It is all here, Baron. The real facts as to the death of old Mrs. Harold, who left you the Blymer estate, which you so rapidly disposed of."

"You are dreaming!"

"And the robbery in the train de-luxe to the Riviera on February 13, 1912. Here is the forged check in the same year on the Credit Lyonnais."

"Tut! You will make nothing of that!"

"Plenty more here, Baron. Here is the complete life history of Miss Minnie Warrender.'"

"No, you are wrong there."

"Then I am right on the others! Now, Baron, you are a card-player. When the other fellow has all the trumps, it saves time to throw down your hand."

"What has all this talk got to do with anything?"

"Gently, Count. Restrain that eager mind! Let me get to the points in my own humdrum fashion. I have all this against you; but, above all, I have a clear case against both you and your comrades in the cases of the attempted gold theft and the missing articles from the treaty."

"Indeed!"

"I have the cabman who took you to Whitehall and the cabman who brought you away. I have the commissionaire who saw you near the case. I have Steiner, who refused to take the rap for you. Steiner has talked, and the game is up."

The veins stood out on the Baron's forehead. His dark, hairy hands were clenched in a convulsion of restrained emotion. He tried to speak, but the words would not shape themselves.

"That is the hand I play from," said Holmes. "I put it all upon the table. But one card is missing. It is the king of diamonds. I want your confession."

"You will never have it."

"No? Now, be reasonable, Count. Consider the situation. You are going to be locked up for at least twenty years. Give me your confession and the law will go easier on you."

"But if I refuse?"

"Why, then--alas!--."

The Baron then had a fine flow of language, and his adjectives were very vigorous. A sudden wild-beast light sprang up in the dark, menacing eyes of the Baron and he ended a string of abuse by a vicious back-hander which Sherlock Holmes failed to entirely avoid. The Baron was out the door and gone in an instant.

In spite of the Count's escape, later that evening their meal was a merry one. Holmes could talk exceedingly well when he chose, and that night he did choose. He appeared to be in a state of nervous exaltation. Watson had never known him so brilliant. He spoke on a quick succession of subjects,—on miracle-plays, on medieval pottery, on Stradivarius violins, on the Buddhism of Ceylon, and on the war-ships of the future,—handling each as though he had made a special study of it. His bright humour marked the reaction from his black depression of the preceding days. Watson felt elated at the thought that they were nearing the end of their task, and he caught something of Holmes's gaiety. Neither of them alluded during dinner to the cause which had brought them to this point.

After dinner Homes went into his bedroom, re-appeared as an old man with a Goatee moustache, and said to Dr. Watson, "Would you chauffer me into the country, my dear Watson?"

The two famous Germans stood beside the stone parapet of the garden walk, with the long, low, heavily gabled house behind them, and they looked down upon the broad sweep of the beach at the foot of the great chalk cliff in which Von Bork, like some wandering eagle, had perched himself four years before. They stood with their heads close together, talking in low, confidential tones. From below the two glowing ends of their cigars might have been the smouldering eyes of some malignant fiend looking down in the darkness.

A remarkable man this Von Bork—a man who could hardly be matched among all the devoted agents of the Kaiser. It was his talents which had first recommended him for the English mission, the most important mission of all, but since he had taken it over those talents had become more and more manifest to the half-dozen people in the world who were really in touch with the truth. One of these was his present companion, Baron von Herling, the chief secretary of the legation, whose huge 100-horse-power Benz car was blocking the country lane as it waited to waft its owner back to London.

"So far as I can judge the trend of events, you will probably be back in Berlin within the week," the secretary was saying. "When you get there, my dear Von Bork, I think you will be surprised at the welcome you will receive. I happen to know what is thought in the highest quarters of your work in this country." He was a huge man, the secretary, deep, broad, and tall, with a slow, heavy fashion of speech which had been his main asset in his political career.

Von Bork laughed.

"They are not very hard to deceive," he remarked. "A more docile, simple folk could not be imagined."

"I do not know about that," said the other thoughtfully. "They have strange limits and one must learn to observe them. It is that surface simplicity of theirs which makes a trap for the stranger. One's first impression is that they are entirely soft. Then one comes suddenly upon something very hard, and you know that you have reached the limit and must adapt yourself to the fact. They have, for example, their insular conventions which simply *must* be observed."

"Meaning 'good form' and that sort of thing?" Von Bork sighed as one who had suffered much.

"Meaning British prejudice in all its queer manifestations. As an example I may quote one of my own worst blunders—I can afford to talk of my blunders, for you know my work well enough to be aware of my successes. It was on my first arrival. I was invited to a week-end gathering at the country house of a cabinet minister. The conversation was amazingly indiscreet."

Von Bork nodded. "I have been there," said he dryly.

"Exactly. Well, I naturally sent a resume of the information to Berlin. Unfortunately our good chancellor is a little heavy-handed in these matters, and he transmitted a remark which showed that he was aware of what had been said. This, of course, took the trail straight up to me. You have no idea the harm that it did me. There was nothing soft about our British hosts on that occasion, I can assure you. I was two years living it down. Now you, with this sporting pose of yours—"

"No, no, do not call it a pose. A pose in an artificial thing. This is quite natural. I am a born sportsman. I enjoy it."

"Well, that makes it the more effective. You yacht against them, you hunt with them, you play polo, you match them in every game, your four-in-hand takes the prize at Olympia. I have even heard that you go the length of boxing with the young officers. What is the result? Nobody takes you seriously. You are a 'good old sport,' 'quite a decent fellow for a German,' a hard-drinking, night-club, knock-about-town, devil-may-care young fellow. And all the time this quiet country house of yours is the centre of half the mischief in England, and the sporting squire the most astute secret-service man in Europe. Genius, my dear Von Bork—genius!"

"You flatter me, Baron. But certainly I may claim my four years in this country have not been unproductive. I have never shown you my little store. Would you mind stepping in for a moment?"

The door of the study opened straight on to the terrace. Von Bork pushed it back, and, leading the way, he clicked the switch of the electric light. He then closed the door behind the bulky form which followed him and carefully adjusted the heavy curtain over the latticed window. Only when all these precautions had been taken and tested did he turn his sunburned aquiline face to his guest.

"Some of my papers have gone," said he. "When my wife and the household left yesterday for Flushing they took the less important with them. I must, of course, claim the protection of the embassy for the others."

"Your name has already been filed as one of the personal suite. There will be no difficulties for you or your baggage. Of course, it is just possible that we may not have to go. England may leave France to her fate. We are sure that there is no binding treaty between them."

"And Belgium?"

"Yes, and Belgium, too."

Von Bork shook his head. "I do not see how that could be. There is a definite treaty there. She could never recover from such a humiliation."

"She would at least have peace for the moment."

"But her honor?"

"Tut, my dear sir, we live in a utilitarian age. Honour is a mediaeval conception. Besides England is not ready. It is an inconceivable thing, but even our special war tax of fifty million, which one would think made our purpose as clear as if we had advertised it on the front page of the *Times*, has not roused these people from their slumbers. Here and there one hears a question. It is my business to find an answer. Here and there also there is an irritation. It is my business to soothe it. But I can assure you that so far as the essentials go—the storage of munitions, the preparation for submarine attack, the arrangements for making high explosives—nothing is prepared. How, then, can England come in, especially when we have stirred her up such a devil's brew of Irish civil war, window-breaking Furies, and God knows what to keep her thoughts at home."

"She must think of her future."

"Ah, that is another matter. I fancy that in the future we have our own definite plans about England, and that your information will be vital to us. It is to-day or to-morrow with Mr. John Bull. If he prefers to-day we are perfectly ready. If it is to-morrow we shall be more ready still. I should think they would be wiser to fight with allies than without them, but that is their own affair. This week is their week of destiny. But you were speaking of your papers." He sat in the armchair with the light shining upon his broad bald head, while he puffed sedately at his cigar.

The large oak-paneled, book-lined room had a curtain hung in the further corner. When this was drawn it disclosed a large, brass-bound safe. Von Bork detached a small key from his watch chain, and after some considerable manipulation of the lock he swung open the heavy door.

"Look!" said he, standing clear, with a wave of his hand.

The light shone vividly into the opened safe, and the secretary of the embassy gazed with an absorbed interest at the rows of stuffed pigeon-holes with which it was furnished. Each pigeon-hole had its label, and his eyes as he glanced along them read a long series of such titles as "Fords," "Harbour-defences," "Aeroplanes," "Ireland," "Egypt," "Portsmouth forts," "The Channel," "Rosythe," and a score of others. Each compartment was bristling with papers and plans.

"Colossal!" said the secretary. Putting down his cigar he softly clapped his fat hands.

"And all in four years, Baron. Not such a bad show for the hard-drinking, hard-riding country squire. But the gem of my collection is coming and there is the setting all ready for it." He pointed to a space over which "Naval Signals" was printed.

"But you have a good dossier there already."

"Out of date and waste paper. The Admiralty in

some way got the alarm and every code has been changed. It was a blow, Baron—the worst setback in my whole campaign. But thanks to my check-book and the good Altamont all will be well to-night."

The Baron looked at his watch and gave a guttural exclamation of disappointment.

"Well, I really can wait no longer. You can imagine that things are moving at present in Carlton Terrace and that we have all to be at our posts. I had hoped to be able to bring news of your great coup. Did Altamont name no hour?"

Von Bork pushed over a telegram.

Will come without fail to-night and bring new rudder.

—Altamont.

"A new rudder, eh?"

"You see he poses as a yachting enthusiast and I keep several boats and a chandlery. In our code everything likely to come up is named after some spare boat part. If he talks of a mast it is a battleship, of a jib a cruiser, and so on. A new rudder refers to naval signals."

"From Portsmouth at midday," said the secretary, examining the superscription. "By the way, what do you give him?"

"Five hundred pounds for this particular job. Of course he has a salary as well."

"The greedy rouge. They are useful, these traitors, but I grudge them their blood money."

"I grudge Altamont nothing. He is a wonderful worker. If I pay him well, at least he delivers the goods, to use his own phrase. Besides he is not a traitor. I assure you that our most pan-Germanic Junker is a sucking dove in his feelings towards England as compared with a real bitter Irish-American."

"Oh, an Irish-American?"

"If you heard him talk you would not doubt it. Sometimes I assure you I can hardly understand him. He seems to have declared war on the King's English as well as on the English king. Must you really go? He may be here any moment."

"No. I'm sorry, but I have already overstayed my time. We shall expect you early to-morrow, and when you get that signal book through the little door on the Duke of York's steps you can put a triumphant finis to your record in England. What! Tokay!" He indicated a heavily sealed dust-covered bottle which stood with two high glasses upon a salver.

"May I offer you a glass before your journey?"

"No, thank you. But it looks like revelry."

"Altamont has a nice taste in wines, and he took a fancy to my Tokay. He is a touchy fellow and needs humouring in small things. I have to study him, I assure you."

They had strolled out on to the terrace again, and along it to the further end where at a touch from the Baron's chauffeur the great car shivered and chuckled.

"Those are the lights of Harwich, I suppose," said the secretary, pulling on his dust coat. "How still and peaceful it all seems. There may be other lights within the week, and the English coast a less tranquil place! The heavens, too, may not be quite so peaceful if all that the good Zeppelin promises us comes true. By the way, who is that?"

Only one window showed a light behind them; in it there stood a lamp, and beside it, seated at a table, was a dear old ruddy-faced woman in a country cap.

She was bending over her knitting and stopping occasionally to stroke a large black cat upon a stool beside her.

"That is Martha, the only servant I have left." The secretary chuckled.

"She might almost personify Britannia," said he, "with her complete self-absorption and general air of comfortable somnolence. Well, *au revoir*, Von Bork!"

With a final wave of his hand he sprang into the car, and a moment later the two golden cones from the headlights shot through the darkness. The secretary lay back in the cushions of the luxurious limousine, with his thoughts so full of the impending European tragedy that he hardly observed that as his car swung round the village street it nearly passed over a little Ford coming in the opposite direction.

Von Bork walked slowly back to the study when the last gleams of the motor lamps had faded into the distance. As he passed he observed that his old housekeeper had put out her lamp and retired. It was a new experience to him, the silence and darkness of his widespread house, for his family and household had been a large one. It was a relief to him, however, to think that they were all in safety and that, but for that one old woman who had lingered in the kitchen, he had the whole place to himself.

There was a good deal of tidying up to do inside his study and he set himself to do it until his keen, handsome face was flushed with the heat of the burning papers. A leather valise stood beside his table, and into this he began to pack neatly and systematically the precious contents of his safe. He had hardly got started with the work, however, when his quick ears caught the sounds of a distant car. Instantly he gave an exclamation of satisfaction, strapped up the valise, shut the safe, locked it, and hurried out on to the terrace. He was just in time to see the lights of a small car come to a halt at the gate. A passenger sprang out of it and advanced swiftly towards him, while the chauffeur, a heavily built, elderly man with a gray moustache, settled down like one who resigns himself to a long vigil.

"Well?" asked Von Bork eagerly, running forward to meet his visitor.

For answer the man waved a small brown-paper parcel triumphantly above his head.

"You can give me the glad hand to-night, mister," he cried. "I'm bringing home the bacon at last."

"The signals?"

"Same as I said in my cable. Every last one of them, semaphore, lamp code, Marconi—a copy, mind you, not the original. That was too dangerous. But it's the real goods, and you can lay to that." He slapped the German upon the shoulder with a rough familiarity from which the other winced.

"Come in," he said. "I am all alone in the house. I was only waiting for this. Of course a copy is better than the original. If an original were missing they would change the whole thing. You think it is all safe about the copy?"

The Irish-American had entered the study and stretched his long limbs from the armchair. He was a tall, gaunt man of sixty, with clear-cut features and a small goatee beard which gave him a general resemblance to the caricatures of Uncle Sam. A half-smoked, sodden cigar hung from the corner of his mouth, and as he sat down he struck a match and relit it.

"Making ready for a move?" he re-marked as he looked round him. "Say, mister," he added, as his eyes fell upon the safe from which the curtain was now removed, "you don't tell me you keep your papers in that?"

"Why not?"

"Gosh, in a wide-open contraption like that! And they reckon you to be some spy. Why, a Yankee crook would be into that with a can-opener. If I'd known that any letter of mine was goin' to lie loose in a thing like that I'd have been a mug to write to you at all."

"It would puzzle any crook to force that safe," Von Bork answered. "You will not cut that metal with any tool."

"But the lock?"

"No, it is a double combination lock. You know what that is?"

"Search me," said the American.

"Well, you need a word as well as a set of figures before you can get the lock to work." He rose and showed a double-radiating disc round the key-hole. "This outer one is for the letters, the inner one for the figures."

"Well, well, that's fine."

"So it's not quite as simple as you thought. It was four years ago that I had it made, and what do you think I chose for the word and figures?"

"It's beyond me."

"Well, I chose August for the word, and 1914 for the figures, and here we are."

The American's face showed his surprise and admiration.

"My, but that was smart! You had it down to a fine thing."

"Yes, a few of us even then could have guessed the date. Here it is, and I am shutting down to-morrow morning."

"Well, I guess you'll have to fix me up also. I'm not staying is this gol-darned country all on my lonesome. In a week or less, from what I see, John Bull will be on his hind legs and fair ramping. I'd rather watch him from over the water."

"But you are an American citizen?"

"Well, so was Jack James an American citizen, but he's doing time in Portland all the same. It cuts no ice with a British copper to tell him you're an American citizen. 'It's British law and order over here,' says he. By the way, mister, talking of Jack James, it seems to me you don't do much to cover your men."

"What do you mean?" Von Bork asked sharply.

"Well, you are their employer, ain't you? It's up to you to see that they don't fall down. But they do fall down, and when did you ever pick them up? There's James—"

"It was James's own fault. You know that yourself. He was too self-willed for the job."

"James was a bonehead—I give you that. Then there was Hollis."

"The man was mad."

"Well, he went a bit woozy towards the end. It's enough to make a man bug-house when he has to play a part from morning to night with a hundred guys all ready to set the coppers wise to him. But now there is Steiner—"

Von Bork started violently, and his ruddy face turned a shade paler.

"What about Steiner?"

"Well, they've got him, that's all. They raided his store, and he and his papers are all in Portsmouth jail. You'll go off and he, poor devil, will have to stand the racket, and lucky if he gets off with his life. That's why I want to get over the water as soon as you do."

Von Bork was a strong, self-contained man, but it

was easy to see that the news had shaken him.

"How could they have got on to Steiner?" he muttered. "That is the worst blow yet."

"Well, you nearly had a worse one, for I believe they are not far off me."

"You do not mean that!"

"Sure thing. My landlady down Fratton way had some inquiries, and when I heard of it I guessed it was time for me to hustle. But what I want to know, mister, is how the coppers know these things? Steiner is the fifth man you've lost since I signed on with you, and I know the name of the sixth if I don't get a move on. How do you explain it, and ain't you ashamed to see your men go down like this?"

Von Bork flushed crimson.

"How dare you speak in such a way!"

"If I didn't dare things, mister, I wouldn't be in your service. But I'll tell you straight what is in my mind. I've heard that with you German politicians when an agent has done his work you are not sorry to see him put away."

Von Bork sprang to his feet.

"Do you dare to suggest that I have given away my own agents!"

"I don't stand for that, mister, but there's a stool pigeon or a cross somewhere, and it's up to you to find out where it is. Anyhow I am taking no more chances. It's me for little Holland, and the sooner the better."

Von Bork had mastered his anger.

"We have been allies too long to quarrel now at the very hour of victory," he said. "You have done splendid work and taken risks, and I cannot forget it. By all means go to Holland, and you can get a boat from Rotterdam to New York. No other line will be safe a week from now. I will take that book and pack it with the rest."

The American held the small parcel in his hand, but made no motion to give it up.

"What about the dough?" he asked.

"The what?"

"The boodle. The reward. The £500. The gunner turned damned nasty at the last, and I had to square him with an extra hundred dollars or it would have been nitsky for you and me. 'Nothin' doin'!' says he, and he meant it, too, but the last hundred did it. It's cost me two hundred pound from first to last, so it isn't likely I'd give it up without gettin' my wad."

Von Bork smiled with some bitterness. "You do not seem to have a very high opinion of my honour," said he, "you want the money before you give up the book."

"Well, mister, it is a business proposition."

"All right. Have your way." He sat down at the table and scribbled a check, which he tore from the book, but he refrained from handing it to his companion. "After all, since we are to be on such terms, Mr. Altamont," said he, "I do not see why I should trust you any more than you trust me. Do you understand?" he added, looking back over his shoulder at the American. "There is the check upon the table. I claim the right to examine that parcel before you pick the money up."

The American passed it over without a word. Von Bork undid a winding of string and two wrappers of paper. Then he sat dazing for a moment in silent amazement at a small blue book which lay before him. Across the cover was printed in golden letters *The life of the Bee by Maurice Masterlinck translated by Alfred Sutro.* Only for one instant did the master spy glare at this strangely irrelevant inscription. The next he was gripped at the back of his neck by a grasp of iron, and a chloroformed sponge was held in front of his writhing face.

"Another glass, Watson!" said Mr. Sherlock Holmes as he extended the bottle of Imperial Tokay.

The thickset chauffeur, who had seated himself by the table, pushed forward his glass with some eagerness.

"It is a good wine, Holmes."

"A remarkable wine, Watson. Our friend upon the sofa has assured me that it is from Franz Josef's special cellar at the Schoenbrunn Palace. Might I trouble you to open the window, for chloroform vapour does not help the palate."

The safe was ajar, and Holmes standing in front of it was removing dossier after dossier, swiftly examining each, and then packing it neatly in Von Bork's valise. The German lay upon the sofa sleeping stertorously with a strap round his upper arms and another round his legs.

"We need not hurry ourselves, Watson. We are safe from interruption. Would you mind touching the bell? There is no one in the house except old Martha, who has played her part to admiration. I got her the situation here when first I took the matter up. Ah, Martha, you will be glad to hear that all is well."

The pleasant old lady had appeared in the door-way. She curtseyed with a smile to Mr. Holmes, but glanced with some apprehension at the figure upon the sofa.

"It is all right, Martha. He has not been hurt at all."

"I am glad of that, Mr. Holmes. According to his lights he has been a kind master. He wanted me to go with his wife to Germany yesterday, but that would hardly have suited your plans, would it, sir?"

"No, indeed, Martha. So long as you were here I was easy in my mind. We waited some time for your signal to-night."

"It was the secretary, sir."

"I know. His car passed ours."

"I thought he would never go. I knew that it would not suit your plans, sir, to find him here."

"No, indeed. Well, it only meant that we waited half an hour or so until I saw your lamp go out and knew that the coast was clear. You can report to me to-morrow in London, Martha, at Claridge's Hotel."

"Very good, sir."

"I suppose you have everything ready to leave."

"Yes, sir. He posted seven letters to-day. I have the addresses as usual."

"Very good, Martha. I will look into them to-morrow. Good-night. These papers," he continued as the old lady vanished, "are not of great importance, for, of course, the information which they represent has been sent off long ago to the German government. These are the originals which cold not safely be got out of the country."

"Then they are of no use."

"I should not go so far as to say that, Watson. They will at least show our people what is known and what is not. I may say that a good many of these papers have come through me, and I need not add are thoroughly untrustworthy. It would brighten my declining years to see a German cruiser navigating the Solent according to the mine-field plans which I have furnished. But you, Watson"—he stopped his work and took his old friend by the shoulders—"I have hardly seen you. You look the same blithe boy as ever."

"I feel twenty years younger, Holmes. I have seldom felt so happy."

"Yet to-morrow it will be but a dreadful memory."

"But this case, Holmes. Tell me what we have

done."

"The fact is, Watson, that this gentleman upon the sofa was a bit too good for our people. He was in a class by himself. Things were going wrong, and no one could understand why they were going wrong. Agents were suspected or even caught, but there was evidence of some strong and secret central force. It was absolutely necessary to expose it. Strong pressure was brought upon me to look into the matter. It has cost me, Watson, but has not been devoid of excitement. When I say that I had to work for some time to eventually catch the eye of a subordinate agent of Von Bork, who recommended me as a likely man, you will realize that the matter was complex. Since then I have been honoured by his confidence, which has not prevented most of his plans going subtly wrong and five of his best agents being in prison. I watched them, Watson, and I picked them as they ripened. Well, sir, I hope that you are none the worse!"

The last remark was addressed to Von Bork him-self, who after much gasping and blinking had lain quietly listening to Holmes's statement. He broke out now into a furious stream of German invective, his face convulsed with passion. Holmes continued his swift investigation of documents while his prisoner cursed and swore.

"Though unmusical, German is the most expressive of all languages," he observed when Von Bork had stopped from pure exhaustion. "Hullo! Hullo!" he added as he looked hard at the corner of a tracing before putting it in the box. "This should put another bird in the cage. I had no idea that the paymaster was such a rascal, though I have long had an eye upon him. Mister Von Bork, you have a great deal to answer for."

The prisoner had raised himself with some difficulty upon the sofa and was staring with a strange mixture of amazement and hatred at his captor.

"I shall get level with you, Altamont," he said, speaking with slow deliberation. "If it takes me all my life I shall get level with you!"

"The old sweet song," said Holmes. "How often have I heard it in days gone by. It was a favorite ditty of the late lamented Professor Moriarty. Colonel Sebastian Moran has also been known to warble it. And yet I live."

"Curse you, you double traitor!" cried the German, straining against his bonds and glaring murder from his furious eyes.

"No, no, it is not so bad as that," said Holmes, smiling. "As my speech surely shows you, Mr. Altamont of Chicago had no existence in fact. I used him and he is gone."

"Then who are you?"

"It is really immaterial who I am, but since the matter seems to interest you, Mr. Von Bork, I may say that this is not my first acquaintance with the members of your family. I have done a good deal of business in Germany in the past and my name is probably familiar to you."

"I would wish to know it," said the Prussian grimly.

"It was I who brought about the separation between Irene Adler and the late King of Bohemia when your cousin Heinrich was the Imperial Envoy. It was I also who saved from murder, by the Nihilist Klopman, Count Von und Zu Grafenstein, who was your mother's elder brother. It was I who recently captured your colleagues Oberstein and Adolph Mayer."

Von Bork sat up in amazement. "There is only one man," he cried.

"Exactly," said Holmes.

Von Bork groaned and sank back on the sofa. "And

most of that information came through you," he cried. "What is it worth? What have I done? It is my ruin forever!"

"It is certainly a little untrustworthy," said Holmes. "It will require some checking and you have little time to check it. Your admiral may find the new guns rather larger than he expects, and the cruisers perhaps a trifle faster."

Von Bork clutched at his own throat in despair.

"There are a good many other points of detail which will, no doubt, come to light in good time. But you have one quality which is very rare in a German, Mr. Von Bork: you are a sportsman and you will bear me no ill-will when you realize that you, who have outwitted so many other people, have at last been outwitted yourself. After all, you have done your best for your country, and I have done my best for mine, and what could be more natural? Besides," he added, not unkindly, as he laid his hand upon the shoulder of the prostrate man, "it is better than to fall before some ignoble foe. These papers are now ready, Watson. If you will help me with our prisoner, I think that we may get started for London at once."

It was no easy task to move Von Bork, for he was a strong and a desperate man. Finally, holding either arm, the two friends walked him slowly down the garden walk which he had trod with such proud confidence when he received the congratulations of the famous diplomatist only a few hours before. After a short, final struggle he was hoisted, still bound hand and foot, into the spare seat of the little car. His precious valise was wedged in beside him.

"I trust that you are as comfortable as circumstances permit," said Holmes when the final arrangements were made. "Should I be guilty of a liberty if I lit a cigar and placed it between your lips?"

But all amenities were wasted upon the angry German.

"I suppose you realize, Mr. Sherlock Holmes," said he, "that if your government bears you out in this treatment it becomes an act of war."

"What about your government and all this treatment?" said Holmes, tapping the valise.

"You are a private individual. You have no warrant for my arrest. The whole proceeding is absolutely illegal and outrageous."

"Absolutely," said Holmes.

"Kidnapping a German subject."

"And stealing his private papers."

"Well, you realize your position, you and your accomplice here. If I were to shout for help as we pass through the village—"

"My dear sir, if you did anything so foolish you would probably enlarge the two limited titles of our village inns by giving us 'The Dangling Prussian' as a signpost. The Englishman is a patient creature, but at present his temper is a little inflamed, and it would be as well not to try him too far. No, Mr. Von Bork, you will go with us in a quiet, sensible fashion to Scotland Yard, whence you can send for your friend, Baron von Herling, and see if even now you may not fill that place which he has reserved for you in the ambassadorial suite. As to you, Watson, stand with me here upon the terrace, for it may be the last quiet talk that we shall ever have."

The two friends chatted in intimate converse for a few minutes, recalling once again the days of the past, while their prisoner vainly wriggled to undo the bonds that held him. As they turned to the car Holmes pointed back to the moonlit sea and shook a thoughtful head.

"There is an east wind coming, Watson."

"I think not, Holmes. It is quite warm."

"Good old Watson! You are the one fixed point in a changing age. There is an east wind coming all the same, such a wind as never blew on England yet. It will be cold and bitter, Watson, and a good many of us may wither before its blast. But it is God's own wind none the less, and a cleaner, better, stronger land will lie in the sunshine when the storm has cleared. Start her up, Watson, for it is time that we were on our way. I have a check for five hundred pounds which should be cashed early, for the drawer is quite capable of stopping it if he can."

Also from MX Publishing

MX Publishing is the world's largest specialist Sherlock Holmes publisher, with over a hundred titles and fifty authors creating the latest in Sherlock Holmes fiction and non-fiction.

From traditional short stories and novels to travel guides and quiz books, MX Publishing cater for all Holmes fans.

The collection includes leading titles such as *Benedict Cumberbatch In Transition* and *The Norwood Author* which won the 2011 Howlett Award (Sherlock Holmes Book of the Year).

MX Publishing also has one of the largest communities of Holmes fans on Facebook with regular contributions from dozens of authors.

www.mxpublishing.com

The Amateur Executioner

London, 1920: Boston-bred Enoch Hale, working as a reporter for the Central Press Syndicate, arrives on the scene shortly after a music hall escape artist is found hanging from the ceiling in his dressing room. What at first appears to be a suicide turns out to be murder . . .

The Enoch Hale and Sherlock Holmes series continues with *The Poisoned Penman* and concludes with *The Egyptian Curse*.

This series brings together two of the most prolific Sherlock Holmes writers of their era – Dan Andriacco and Kieran McMullen.

Also from MX Publishing

"Phil Growick's, *'The Secret Journal of Dr Watson'*, is an adventure which takes place in the latter part of Holmes and Watson's lives. They are entrusted by HM Government (although not officially) and the King no less to undertake a rescue mission to save the Romanovs, Russia's Royal family from a grisly end at the hand of the Bolsheviks. There is a wealth of detail in the story but not so much as would detract us from the enjoyment of the story. Espionage, counter-espionage, the ace of spies himself, double-agents, double-crossers...all these flit across the pages in a realistic and exciting way. All the characters are extremely well-drawn and Mr Growick, most importantly, does not falter with a very good ear for Holmesian dialogue indeed. Highly recommended. A five-star effort."
The Baker Street Society

The characters return in the sequel *'The Revenge of Sherlock Holmes'*.

www.ingramcontent.com/pod-product-compliance
Lightning Source LLC
Chambersburg PA
CBHW071306130626
46556CB00004B/1496